THE LUTE PLAYER

THE HERZBERG TRILOGY

The Music Book

A young English woman, on the run from her father, and a retired Prussian military officer sent to England by King Frederick the Great are plunged into the London demi-monde and a pursuit across Europe in search of fulfilment. The young woman's music book bears witness to what unfolds.

Fortune's Sonata

English by birth, Prussian by marriage, rebellious by nature, the beautiful Arabella von Deppe steers her family through turbulent historical times in this thrilling story of love and loss, betrayal and revenge, ambition and beliefs, friendship and fate. With music as her inspiration and a murderer as her friend, she proves a worthy adversary of Fortune as she weathers winds beyond her control.

A Motif of Seasons

Two powerful 19th-century English and Prussian families are still riven by the consequences of an ancestral marriage – one that bequeathed venomous division, rivalry and hatred. Three beautiful women – each ambitious and musically gifted – seek to break these inherited shackles of betrayal, revenge and cruelty in their pursuit of sexual freedom and love. But the past proves a formidable and vicious opponent.

* * *

The Executioner's House

Germany, October 1946. The Nuremburg war crimes tribunal has just ended. Major Richard Fortescue, previously part of the British prosecution team, is returning to London when he encounters Karin Eilers, a young German woman with a dark past. Against the backdrop of war-devastated Berlin and the continuing search for former Nazis, their brief affair and a mysterious black notebook make them unwitting pawns in a deadly game of intrigue and betrayal played by British and Soviet intelligence. What wartime secrets will the notebook unravel? Who else will become a victim of the battle for its possession?

THE
Lute Player

EDWARD GLOVER

Published by The Oak House
High Street, Thornham, Norfolk PE36 6LY

ISBN: 978-0-9929551-4-4

Dedicated to Khadra in Palestine

For Orpheus' lute was strung with poets' sinews,

Whose golden touch could soften steel and stones,

Make tigers tame and huge leviathans

Forsake unsounded deeps to dance on sands.

William Shakespeare

The Two Gentlemen of Verona Act III Scene 2

CONTENTS

PART ONE

Johannes' Story

CHAPTER ONE

Journey Through the Night

It was February, with no respite from winter's long encore of darkness and bone-numbing cold. For the ninth consecutive day, the chilling north wind blew. The harbour was frozen, vessels locked in ice. The cathedral's great bell rang out the late hour of the evening.

He stepped outside, light and warmth behind, ahead only immuring gloom beneath a remote multitude of stars. Everything was silent, except in the distance soft, beguiling fragments of music carried on a glacial wind and the crunch of the deep frost beneath his feet. He looked back. The light he had left had become a mere speck. He paused for a moment. Should he turn on his heel and return to predictability and the chatter of voices, or walk on? He listened again. The music had become more distinct, more persistent, more alluring. The choice was inevitable. He blew harder on already throbbing hands, pulled the collar of his coat more tightly around his neck and walked on. He stumbled more than once on the icy cobbles but each time regained his balance as he trudged further along the dark street. The music became louder, the melody clearer, more insistent.

He reached an imposing wooden door, its pointed arch multiplied in the ornate mouldings of the surrounding masonry. Hesitant, unsure, he turned the heavy handle, pushed hard and entered, the door creaking on its ancient hinges. He halted, but lured by the mellifluous sound he edged forwards, his footsteps on the uneven stone floor echoing in the vastness of the black space around him. Though he could not see its source, the music became stronger and ever sweeter, drawing him on. He walked a few paces then stopped. He could hear but still could not see in the blinding darkness. He became uneasy, sensing he was on the edge of a precipice and that if he ventured further he might fall headlong into a bottomless pit. His courage beginning to ebb, he was about to retrace his steps when suddenly he saw a small candle flame flickering in the distance. Cold, insecure and fearful, he nonetheless summoned the resolve to inch towards the light, the music becoming his guide. As he drew nearer to the expanding flame – quivering colours of yellow, red and blue in agitated motion – he saw the form of a hooded figure, its fingers plucking at the strings of a lute. The shape of the instrument was unusual – swelling, organic, gourdlike. He stood motionless, transfixed by the rich, sweet melody. For how long he remained there, he could not say.

Suddenly, the figure leaned towards the candle, revealing its face. For a moment, it appeared to be that of a handsome young man, but, moving closer, he saw it was not. It was the face of a young girl. She looked up and smiled at him. As she did so, the candle burned even brighter, and in its circumference of light he noticed a rough-hewn bench close by. He sat down, enveloped in the stillness surrounding him, warmed by the flame and mesmerised by the music. The girl stopped to draw the candle nearer to her; her cloak rustled, its hood slipping back. Long, deep-golden hair tumbled free around her small face onto her shoulders. Again she smiled at him and gathered her cloak over her gown of red russet. He tried to speak but the child put her finger to her lips to hush him. She began to play once more, her features now obscured by her waves of hair. He sat back, closing his eyes, entranced by the music which seemed to be weaving a rich fabric of coloured patterns around him. The air was perfumed with the sweetest of scents, almost intoxicating in their intensity.

Sensing through his closed eyelids a surge in the candle's brightness he opened his eyes just as the notes of the lute gave way to another instrument. An organ sprang into life, proclaiming its mighty power in unceasing torrents of flamboyant sound, filling the emerging immensity of a mighty Gothic cathedral. The pulsating music was matched by great shafts of light penetrating the ancient glass windows, bringing alive images of saints and martyrs. Above the nave, a gargoyle, its face fixed in a grotesque stare, suddenly broke free. Grimacing with evident pain from the bellowing organ pipes, it scuttled away into the far darkness, its hands pressed hard against its pointed ears. The devil's incarnation, it could not bear the music from an instrument declaring deafening victory over despair. As the last notes of the toccata receded, to be replaced by the gentler, higher notes of a fugue, angelic figures stepped from the roof bosses to sway to the ensuing adagio. He looked at the statue of the Virgin. For a fleeting moment, he thought he saw her foot – pressed on the serpent beneath her sandal – tap to the rhythm of the heavenly melody. He gazed towards the altar and beyond, to where the huge east window should have been, but in its place was cosmic infinity, illuminated by an array of stars, some dim and some almost dancing in their brightness.

Suddenly, the organ ceased, leaving only diminishing echoes rippling through the arches along each side of the nave. As the beams of light also decreased in intensity, the cathedral's architecture slowly disappeared into impenetrable darkness, with only the single candle once again providing illumination. The lutenist resumed her playing. As he sat gazing at her, lulled by her music, he sensed the ground beneath him beginning to give way. Yet he felt no fear. The musical fabric in which he was now wrapped gave him the sensation of floating, as though he was now on a boat tugging gently at its painter. He became aware of a dark-clothed figure behind him, standing in the boat's stern, untying the mooring rope. Suddenly, above the open deck, he heard the loud crack of a sail bursting free from its bindings, the thud and creak as it quickly filled with a wind that was gathering in strength. The boat rocked lightly as it slipped out into the inky blackness.

In the bow of the craft sat the child, her face half illuminated by the lantern behind her, swinging in the warm night currents that had supplanted the Arctic blasts. As before she smiled at him and began to sing a sweet lullaby in some foreign tongue he did not recognise. He wanted to speak, to ask her name and where they were going. But he was mute; no words came. He lay back, weighed down by a fatigue he could not resist. He closed his eyes, without fear of the night, and as she continued to sing and pluck easeful notes from her lute, the helmsman steered the boat further into the blackness. He could no longer resist sleep. In the past, he had often been plagued by dreams – some odd, some troubling, and some so perplexing that they lingered in his consciousness the next day. But now his sleep was peaceful, unblemished by fears and the inexplicable. Several times he stirred, but what he saw remained calmingly the same: the girl playing her lute softly beneath the lantern as their craft sailed silently across an unseen sea through a realm of endless darkness, with no stars, only a narrow crescent of moon to guide the way, no distant landmarks to define the boundaries of this jet-dense nothingness. Once on waking, he again heard the girl quietly singing in a language he could not recognise. And then in words he could understand:

> *She sent her likeness stealing in dream*
> *to him who waking would not be appeased.*
> *But her phantom found no favour with mine,*
> *which stood its ground, unmoved by complaint.*
> *You fancied my phantom a shade too light*
> *anger to feel at what angers me so.*
> *Ask not for a truce so soon, Jinan,*
> *for the things you did were far from a dream.*

He was adrift, but with no concern as to where he might be going and oblivious to the claims of the past. As he slipped yet once more into irresistible sleep, he could still vaguely remember the origins of his passage – walking towards the music he had heard on the wind. Yet as the boat rocked rhythmically in the lulling waves lapping its hull, he had no care for its destination.

The journey through the night seemed endless, no sound save the gentle flap of the sail in the warm westerly wind and the susurrating brush of water. After what felt like many hours' rest, he woke again. It was still dark. He turned to look at the boatman in the stern, his sunken cheeks shadowed by the dim lantern behind him. In the bow, the girl was no longer playing. Her cloak wrapped tightly around her, her back to him and her lute close beside her, she gazed into the distance. Hearing him stir, she turned; he saw no smile, only tears. He looked beyond her silhouette but saw nothing. Remaining awake, he continued his watch. Surely, before long, this journey must emerge into the light of day. Peering harder, he saw a thin line of lustre on the horizon, as though a fire-tipped arrow were streaking across the distant firmament. Within minutes, from the arrow's trail the glow in the eastern sky widened, bathing the boat and the sea about them in a rich tapestry of blue and green hues.

"We will be there within the hour," said the boatman.

At his words, the child picked up her lute and began to play – not a pleasing melody as before, but mournful notes.

CHAPTER TWO

Journey Inland

The boat ran aground on the soft shore. Two olive-skinned men, lines of age etched deeply into their faces, appeared from behind the dunes and helped drag the craft clear of the water. The boatman said nothing. The lute player, grasping an outstretched hand, stepped from the boat and walked up the sand, followed by the two men. She turned to look at the passenger still aboard. Two other men came and stood beside her. The taller of these cupped his hands to his mouth.

"You. Come. You cannot stay there. We are to guide you on your journey inland."

"But I do not wish to go," I called back.

"You must," implored the lute player. "If you do not come with us, your journey will never finish and mine too will remain incomplete."

"I must go back. That is my homeland," I insisted, pointing out to sea. "That is where I wish to return, not travel further east."

"You will go back one day. But not now, not today. So, please come. I beg you," she said, her voice gently beseeching me.

The shorter of the two men returned to the water's edge, the girl at his side. He approached the boat, holding out his hand.

"Come. We are wasting time. The sun will soon be high in the sky. There is no shade here and it will shortly be too hot to travel. The more we linger, the more difficult our journey will be."

Once more he proffered his hand.

"I will come with you too. You will have no regrets," the lute player said.

I hesitated, but seeing a further imploring look on the young girl's face I stepped unsteadily from the boat. She took my arm and with repeated urging from the two men we stumbled slowly, falteringly, between the grass-flecked dunes. With the shore receding behind us, we quickened our pace. I looked back. Only the boatman was left, unfurling the sail as the craft edged out towards the open sea. He waved.

"I will always be here," he called, his words carried on the wind.

And thus began our journey inland, on mules, taking three days to cross a dusty plain and its villages, towards mountains in the distance. On the fourth day, we began our ascent through rocky foothills. The air became cooler and the sky a deeper blue. As the incline became steeper, so our progress became slower. Some days later – I had lost count – we arrived at a village, somewhat larger than those through which we had previously passed, and close to the shore of a great lake. Behind the village lay the ruins of a Roman settlement, pillars tumbled hither and thither as though smitten down in rage by a giant hand.

"Here we will stay for a while," said the tall guide.

"You can rest. Judge what you see and then decide," said one of the men who had helped pull the boat from the water.

"Decide what?" I, the reluctant traveller, replied.

"Decide whether to remain or to return whence you came."

"Why have you brought me all this way to make such a decision? What is the purpose?"

"To see, to learn, to judge," answered the tall guide.

And so I stayed. I discovered, through observation and questions – often more sign language than words – that the large lake near the village was the Sea of Galilee. The days were warm, the soothing sun easing my weary limbs, sometimes even hot. But the nights brought bitter cold. I walked, frequently alone, to the lake shore to watch the fishermen at work – patching their nets, counting their harvest and haggling with buyers. Ambling along the grey sand, I often recalled what I had left behind. I longed to write and draw, but had no paper, no quill and ink or materials. All I could do was to memorise thoughts and images and how I would refine them once seated at a desk. Each evening, we sat after dusk around the edge of the fire and, after listening to stories set to music, which I slowly began to understand were culled from ancient legends, we stretched out on mats of plaited straw and, wrapped in heavy blankets, gazed up at the stars.

Several days after our arrival I woke earlier than usual, just as the sun rose above the rugged horizon, its warmth touching my cheeks. As the hubbub of daily conversation began, I heard the girl singing, a mournful song, interspersed with quiet sobs. It had been some time since I had seen her, for most days she wandered off along the shore, oblivious to time, her travelling companions and the villagers. Now, she had returned, but was sitting apart, looking out across the lake with her cloak tightly wrapped around her and her face partially obscured by her hood. The lute lay silent beside her. When she heard my voice as I joined the others in our daily breakfast of honey, yoghurt and crisply baked bread, she turned and moved closer to us. The villagers urged her to play a welcome to the new day. As she did so, I watched closely the ravishing skill with which her youthful fingers plucked the strings, sublimely transporting us into pleasurable melancholy and then, with a sudden quickening of tempo, turning our spirits and senses towards places of joy. Next, in a climax of divine musical frenzy, she drove us into an ecstatic mood. Without a pause, amid a fervour of shouting and clapping, she played to such a point that those around her leapt to their feet and began to dance. The head villager suddenly called out.

"Enough. Now we must work."

Later, by midday, we all withdrew to the shade. Seeing me alone, she came and sat beside me, sipping some water.

"What is your name?" I asked. "After all this time I still don't know."

"Why do you want to know?"

"When I travel I like to know the names of my companions. As we have journeyed together in a boat through the night, and trekked side by side many miles inland, and also as you are such an accomplished player of the lute, I wish particularly to know yours."

"The instrument is an oud. As for my name, I do not know who I am. The name I will tell you is the one given to me, after they brought me here, by the man and his wife who have cared for me."

"And what is that name?"

"It is Khadra. It means green, a holy colour, and the colour of the dress I was wearing when they found me."

I looked at her, as if her name might help me see her clearly for the first time. She was young, gentle in appearance, her face pale-skinned, unlike the darker complexion of most of the womenfolk in the village; her hair rich and golden in colour. Her eyes were dark, revealing both sadness and a lively disposition.

"Who are 'they' who found and brought you here?"

For answer she pointed to a group of men and women resting in the mouth of a cave.

"When?" I asked.

"It was long ago, when I was a small child. They found me alone on the beach – the same beach where our boat landed – amongst the wreckage of a ship. Beside me was that." She indicated a large, oblong leather box.

"What is in it?" I asked.

"An instrument like the one I play each day. It was a gift, from a stranger."

"Would you show it to me?"

She opened the box. Inside was a lute of the sort I had often seen played before.

"Do you play it?"

"Sometimes," she replied. "But they prefer me to play this smaller one, the oud."

"Were there others with you on the beach?"

"No. I was alone. They said the others had perished in the sea."

"Do you have any recollection of your early childhood, the time before you were found? Of your parents?"

"Little," she replied. "I remember that my father used to work in a special room, and did not like to be disturbed. Sometimes, I would peer through the keyhole and glimpse pictures, a wooden trestle, shelves filled with coloured bottles, tools strewn on every surface. Once, the door was ajar. I began to push it open. But when he heard the door creak, he chastised me. In that fleeting moment, all I can remember seeing was his back, his rich, dark, uncombed hair reaching in waves to his shoulders, and his green tunic. That is all. I don't remember ever seeing his face."

"And can you recall your mother?"

"If she were my mother, I was barely aware of her. Mostly, I only heard her footsteps, though I vaguely recall occasionally seeing her leave the house early in the morning, never turning to say goodbye. She would return after I had gone to bed, never coming in to say goodnight. Instead, I was looked after by the servants, though they were always busy with their main chores. Sometimes a young man would come and play an instrument like the one in the box, and sing to her. She liked that, as did I. It made her smile – otherwise a rare occurrence. One day he brought me a lute – a child's lute. He taught me some notes. Then not long after, he never came as he promised he would. My mother was unhappier than ever and said I had caused him not to come. From that moment on, or so the servants claimed, the child's lute was played with an adult's melancholy. I remember feeling that the stranger's lute was free from sadness, a gift of pure generosity. That's why I cherished it so dearly, and still do."

Disturbed by her account, I was about to ask Khadra another question when she pulled from beneath her gown a small wooden locket, fastened to a chain she wore around her slender neck. She opened it and turned it towards me. It was an image of the Virgin and Child.

"Do you know who that is?" I asked.

She looked intently at it.

"A woman here once said it was my mother, holding me. One day I would like to find her. She has such a gentle face."

"Who gave you this locket?"

"I do not know. Those who rescued me said it was bound tightly in a piece of oilcloth and on this chain around my neck. I keep it as a memento of who I might really be."

I could not bear to tell her it was not her and her mother but an image of the Holy Mother and the Infant Jesus. I changed the subject.

"Where did you learn to play the lute?"

"The people here taught me. I have played it for as long as I can remember. And there was once an oud player who visited for a while. They said he was famous in the region. He taught me too."

"The melodies you play – where do they come from?"

"From hereabouts – music the shepherds play," she replied.

"Play for me – just a little, and perhaps on the one in the box."

She gently took the lute from its leather case and played. After a while she stopped.

"And you – tell me about you."

"There is little to say. I have travelled. I have stayed in many different places in search of elusive happiness. I have expressed opinions. I enjoy the pleasure of music. It distracts me. But why I am here ... I cannot fathom, except that it was your music that drew me to where I found you."

She smiled.

"And your name? You must tell me your name."

"My name is Johannes."

"Which land do you come from?"

"It is far from here – in the north, where it is achingly cold in the winter."

She started playing again. Then after a few bars she suddenly stopped.

"It's an accident of fate that you and I are here – flung randomly together like grains of sand on the seashore, all part of the ebb and flow of life."

I was taken aback by her words. I judged she could only be thirteen or fourteen in age, yet the philosophical resignation of what she had said displayed a maturity and wisdom beyond her years.

More weeks passed. I watched the lake, its waters sometimes placid but sometimes much agitated by sudden storms of wind and sand, very like the river of life. Occasionally, I sailed in a fishing boat to the middle of the Sea to observe more clearly the distant hills beyond. On another day, I found some rough scraps of paper and with a stub of charcoal from the fire sketched some images of the tumbledown Roman ruin and recorded some brief observations. At other times, I rode with the men into the countryside. Each evening, we would return to gather round the fire and listen to stories of ancient Arabs and to Khadra's music. The weeks became months. The sun grew hotter; sometimes the heat of the day was unbearable.

Eventually, the day came when I knew it was time for me to leave, to return to the coast in hope that the boatman might again be there, ready to take me back. I was sure I was not being held against my will and that it was therefore unlikely I would meet resistance in my endeavour. So I asked to go. The head of the village, Khalid, the man Khadra referred to as her father, smiled.

"Of course you should go. I will choose a guide to lead you back to the great sea. But I must warn you that if the boatman who brought you is not there, you may have to wait many years before he returns."

"However long he may take to return, I will wait."

"And with infinite patience. For that is all you can do. Each of us awaits our fate. Only he knows the way," Khalid replied.

And thus it was decided that within the week I would leave, accompanied by Bassem, one of the men who had guided us inland. The night before our departure, Khadra came to see Khalid and me – not to sing, but to ask to join me on my journey.

"Your place is here, with your mother," said Khalid.

"She is not my mother. This is my mother," replied Khadra, opening the locket. "She is my mother and I wish to find her. Please let me go."

Khalid looked at her. His eyes could not conceal his sorrow. Scarcely able to control his emotion, he took her hand in his.

"Your leaving will pain me and your mother. She has cared for you since you were a small child. But if it be the will of Allah, then you must go. Yet please know this. Whatever you may say, and even if you find your true mother, you will forever be our daughter.

Just play once more for me this evening, so I might have a lasting memory."

Khadra kissed his hand. Khalid, his weather-beaten face full of anguish, turned to me.

"Sir, I entrust this child to you. She means as much to me as to her mother. Care for her, protect her and help her to find the happiness she seeks. I pray that her music will flourish and delight others, as it has brought us great joy. When the wind blows from the west, I will listen for the echo of her songs."

Khadra played for him. When she finished, she handed him the oud.

"Keep this in memory of me."

Khalid was unable to hold back his tears.

The next morning, Bassem, our guide, Khadra and I rode out of the village, leaving behind the ageing man and woman who had cared for Khadra and declared their loving bond in giving her the female version of her father's name. She shed no tears, any emotion she may have felt masked by an outward determination to begin her quest. We headed south-west and then south. I was resolved to return to my country to tell a remarkable story. Beside me was Khadra, now in my care, set on discovering her past. I knew that the journey on which we had embarked would not be easy.

CHAPTER THREE

Lost

As I had anticipated, the trek to the coast was long, circuitous – often veering in different directions – and difficult. We travelled by mule and, when they became tired, on foot, Bassem in front, Khadra either following or alongside him with her lute slung nonchalantly across her back, and me behind. Sometimes Khadra ran excitedly ahead until she was almost out of sight. Bassem called out for her to wait, warning of unexpected danger. Like a child, she stopped teasingly, pausing for us to reach her. Then when we were within touching distance she would once more run ahead, turn and look back towards us, laughing.

We travelled for six or seven hours each day, beginning early in the morning shortly after sunrise, resting in the shade in the midday heat and by four o'clock finding a place to lodge for the night. Our evening meal was frugal, usually some bread, fruit, occasionally a few morsels of lamb, and goat's milk, and then, to the delight of our fellow travellers – we seldom had the route to ourselves – Khadra would play sweet melodies or sing and even sometimes dance around our brightly burning fire, which hungrily consumed wood Bassem had patiently collected earlier in the day. It was often well into the night before we would let Khadra rest. Frequently, we would sleep in a cave, shared with others, or from time to time beneath the trees. I often tried to count the stars through the branches but never got far before I fell asleep.

One morning, well into our journey, we stopped by a large pool to slake our thirst and refill our goatskin bottles. I caught my reflection in the still water – a bearded face with sunken cheeks framed in long, uncombed hair almost down to my shoulders. I sprang back in horror at the aged image. Yet, though the daily mileage was taking its physical toll, my spirits were undimmed. I was returning to the coast, to the boat that would take me home. Bassem said little each day, always looking silently into the distance, vigilant for some unknown danger. Like mine, Khadra's spirit, too, was undimmed. And she was no longer a child. As the days passed, she became taller and more self-assured, with a young woman's beauty beginning to emerge like the rays of the sun from behind a cloud.

The next day we woke early as usual and within an hour or so began walking uphill, an even steeper incline than before.

"How much longer to the coast?" I asked Bassem.

He said nothing, continuing to look ahead towards the line of hills on the horizon. I asked him again. He turned to me, his face, weather-beaten by habitual journeying, edged by his keffiyeh, dark eyes darting, lips pinched, his manner watchful but fearsome, his back straight.

"Shorter than the distance we have come."

"What places are left to pass through before we see the sea?"

"Not many after that one," he replied, pointing to somewhere beyond my sight.

"And what place is that?"

"You will soon discover," he said.

"Will we pause there?"

"Yes," said Bassem. "We will stay there only a day or so to refresh ourselves. No more days than the number of fingers on my right hand."

I looked at his hand. There were only three fingers. He smiled.

"That's right. No more than three days, if you and the young woman wish to reach the coast before the autumn comes and to find the boatman. You must not linger where we will arrive shortly. Beware of the city and its wiles. It is easier to arrive there than to leave. Even its stones are riddled with guile and deception. Nothing is quite what it seems."

We walked on. In the late afternoon, we crested the hill and gazed at the sight below – the city of Jerusalem, a huddled mass of buildings glowing beneath the setting sun, its rays penetrating a ragged bank of clouds strung low across the horizon. Bassem did not speak as we began our descent, Khadra close on his heels; I was two or three steps behind. At dusk, we entered the city through one of its massive gates, mingling with merchants and camels. I had read many books as a child about this city whose beginning was lost in the mists of antiquity. At school, a priest had spoken of Abraham, the prophets and Herod. At home, I devoured stories about the Romans in Jerusalem, whose occupation had been followed by Persians, Arabs, the Crusaders and then the Ottomans, who had rebuilt the city's walls. Now I was within those walls.

It was nightfall by the time we arrived at the city's bustling heart. The narrow, cobbled streets pulsed with people, shouting in different languages, pushing and jostling between the stalls of the traders. Khadra and I followed Bassem closely. He walked with purpose, turning one way and then another. He would frequently look back to check that we were still behind him. On and on we went until we came to a small passageway. Halfway along on the left was an even smaller alley. Near the end on the right, a large, ancient wooden door was set into a high wall. Bassem banged the heavy round ring on its iron plate, calling out as he did so. No one came. He called again and banged his fists on the door. It was slowly opened by a hooded, elderly man who beckoned us to enter. We stepped into a small courtyard, its walls covered in heavily scented bougainvillea punctuated by lanterns. As the door closed behind us, the noise of the nearby streets subsided to a distant murmur.

In the far corner was a short flight of stone steps leading up to a smaller wooden door. The doorkeeper led the way, Bassem first, then Khadra, then me. He opened the door and we went inside.

"Welcome to my house," said a middle-aged woman.

"Greetings," replied Bassem, with an Arabic salutation to which I had become accustomed over the past weeks. He introduced Khadra and me. "We have come from far inland. Our journey has taken many days and my companions are weary. They wish to accept your kind and generous hospitality and to rest, but neither they nor I will stay long as we are on our way to the coast to find a boat to take them across the sea towards the north."

The woman smiled.

"My name is Saida. I have been expecting you. You are most welcome in this house that has gladly opened its doors for centuries. It has seen many travellers and warriors. Here you can rest your weary feet and sleep in comfort. I live alone, so nothing will disturb you except the sound of bells or the call to prayer. Mukhtar will show you where each of you will sleep."

The hooded man stepped forward and we followed him along a covered walkway, each of us entering the room assigned to us.

I washed my face and sore feet in cool, scented water. I was tempted to lie on the neatly made bed but instead, hearing the sound of Khadra's lute, I returned to the room we had first entered and then to the courtyard where she sat, quietly playing music I had not heard before.

The exterior architecture of the house was solid and unremarkable. The courtyard was not particularly striking either, except for the fragrant bougainvillea and the plash of water from a small fountain set into the wall. The main room, where we later sat on stools to eat, was beautifully appointed, with elegant, carved furniture and highly polished brass ornaments. On the walls hung large squares of Arab cloth with images of beasts in a forest. In one corner was a raised dais on which stood a high-backed chair, almost like a throne. Saida saw me looking at it.

"That is where my late husband sat to read," she said, sadness in her voice. "I hope that Khadra will sit there – perhaps tomorrow – and play to us."

After we had eaten, she took us up to the roof. The sky was full of dazzling stars against a deep, almost translucent blue. Across to the right was the dome of the Church of the Holy Sepulchre and below us a sprawling tumble of houses, streets and alleyways.

We returned to the large room to drink tea.

"Now you must sleep," said Saida. "Tomorrow, rise early and see what befalls you."

Bassem left first. I wanted to wait a while longer to hear Khadra, who was sitting in the high-backed chair and almost inaudibly playing her lute. But Saida gently took my arm.

"No, my friend, you are weary. You must go to sleep now. You have much to do to fulfil your shared destiny. Khadra will soon follow once she has played a refrain loved by my husband, recalling the fame of Saladin."

I left the two alone and within a short while was asleep.

The next day Khadra was preparing to explore the city.

"May I come with you?" I asked, unwilling to be without a companion in the house.

She smiled.

"Of course, why should you not?"

"Take care of her," said Saida. "She's an enchantress."

Within the hour we left the small, perfumed walled garden – paradise, Khadra called it – the lute once more slung across her back. She wore an unadorned black abaya, undone at the front from the waist down, and beneath it, a long, red undergown, given to her by Saida, which reached to her ankles and could be seen in flashes of scarlet as she strode along, though the wide embroidered gold band at its top remained hidden. Her long loose hair tumbled from the hood of the abaya.

We walked along narrow streets and down sunless alleyways, passing from Christian quarter to Arab quarter to Jewish quarter, each one crammed with buyer-swarmed stalls. The fruit, the spices, the fabrics on display were rich, colourful and almost liquid in the way they intertwined, in contrast to the harsh, jagged cries of the sellers seeking to attract the attention of passers-by. For a short while, the enigmatic Bassem had followed us, but soon he slipped from sight, nowhere to be seen. As we walked, Khadra's hood slid further back, and the cord around her waist loosened to reveal more of the red garment beneath. From time to time, when older women muttered as she passed, she pulled the black abaya around her once more and the hood back over her head. But before long both would slip again.

We turned another corner, to be confronted by a dispute between two stallholders competing over price. A crowd had gathered around them, expressing their own vigorous opinions. Khadra paused to look at the contentious merchandise. I was suddenly jostled and knocked aside, falling backwards against a wall. Regaining my balance, I pushed through the crowd, expecting to see Khadra still at the stall, but she had disappeared. I ran down the street, and as I passed each intersection I looked left and right in case I could see her. But I soon realised I had lost her.

For the inscrutable Bassem to vanish was unfortunate, but for me to lose my young companion was a fateful blow. It was now gone midday and the sun was high in the sky. It was hot and as I ran this way and that, searching for Khadra, I began to panic. Where was she? Was she all right? How would I find my way back to Saida's house? I was stranded, in limbo, surrounded by strangers whose language I could not speak. A fruit seller, seeing my obvious distress, offered me a drink. I declined as I had no money to pay him. I pressed on along the main street, increasingly concerned, past a church and on towards a temple. Still I could not see her. I sat down on a stone bench, trying desperately to think where she might be. I concluded that to trace where Khadra might have gone was like plotting the flight of a fly. I must have fallen asleep in the midday heat, and for some hours, because when I stirred the sun was already beginning to sink, its rays penetrating an ancient archway through which mules laden with goods were passing.

As dusk approached, I began to walk downhill, trying to remember the way to Saida's – had we walked *up*hill that morning? – to recall some of the merchants I had passed whose stalls I might use as landmarks. Nearing a fork in the narrowing road, I caught sight of a fat-bellied man, a seller of opulently coloured cloth. Like the fruit seller, seeing my evident distress, he took me by the hand and guided me into his shop, nestled behind the trestle tables freighted with bales of cloth, asking me my name and where I was from as he did so. He ushered me to a sofa at the rear of the shop, wedged between yet more bales of sumptuously coloured cloth stacked floor to ceiling.

Establishing a language in which we could speak, I endeavoured to explain my journey to and, God willing, from his land.

"Did you come alone?"

"No. I travelled in a boat steered by a helmsman whose face I rarely saw and a young girl who played the oud."

"I see." He nodded. "We will find her. For now, rest here."

"But I must get to the house belonging to the widow Saida. She may be there."

"I doubt she will be. Besides, I do not know this woman Saida."

"But surely you must know her?"

"I do not know her or her house," he insisted. "Please, rest here. I assure you, all will be well."

I sipped a thick, sweet-tasting fruit juice which he poured from an elaborate ceramic pitcher and ate some small pieces of meat and fish from a platter he placed before me. He showed me samples of his cloth, from which he claimed he had made robes for an emperor, a sultan and a pope.

"My name is Abd al Bari, servant of the wise – but also of the rich. I am a famous trader of cloth and a widely acknowledged tailor of garments. Everyone knows me." Holding up some gold-threaded fabric, he said he could dress me like a king. He offered me another, different drink. I drank it and began to feel overcome with sleep.

"Close your eyes, my friend. Tomorrow we will find your young companion."

I slept a fitful night, full of worries, uneasy dreams of walking along a road towards dark and menacing mountains. I seemed lost in a maze of time.

When I woke the next morning, my host was sitting at a trestle table.

"Come, join me and eat. Then I will freshen you."

As we ate and drank milk, he told me of the many travellers he had met, in the city and beyond. Though prolix, he amused me and I began to enjoy our conversation.

Afterwards, I bathed in a raised pool on a small walled patio behind his shop. Then he shaved me, cut my hair and gave me a long blue-and-white-striped gown to put on and a keffiyeh to protect my head from the sun.

Once his young assistant arrived, together they opened the shop's shutters and placed samples of cloth on the trestle tables outside. The haggling with early buyers began immediately.

"Now," he said, "let us find Khadra."

"How do you know her name?"

"You called out to her often in your sleep."

And so, we began – Abd al Bari and I – to search along the streets and alleyways.

"Stay close to me, Mister Johannes. I do not wish to lose you."

The hubbub in the main thoroughfares was deafening, the straitened alleys full of people, even more numerous than the day before, pushing and shoving. Twice I almost lost sight of him as he strode ahead, turning every which way but with certainty, seeming to know where he was going, taking us up an ever-steeper incline. The street narrowed. He suddenly stopped and seized my arm.

"Do you hear?" he asked.

"Hear what?" I replied.

"The sound of a lute – not an Arab oud but a lute from another land."

I struggled to hear but caught only the noise of the crowd around me. Still gripping my arm, he pushed me forwards a few paces.

"Now can you hear?"

I strained my ears and then suddenly I heard the sound.

"We've found her. Come this way."

We pressed deep into the crowd, squeezing through a gap, barely the width of a man, in a wall that must have been many centuries old. Then I saw her, sitting on the plinth of a broken column, playing her lute, surrounded by women and children. I stood and watched her, fascinated, Abd al Bari equally so. She looked up at me and smiled. As she did, I saw that she had changed, almost beyond recognition, taller and older. Her earlier vulnerability had vanished. Her hair, free of the hood of her abaya, was no longer pure golden but streaked with darker shades. And the music she played was no longer Arab as I had heard so often before on the boat and during our time beside the lake. It was more familiar music, much as I had heard in the past, before my journey began. How could she have changed so much since yesterday? Was I in a different realm of time?

With a gesture of farewell, Abd took his leave and stole away, leaving me to listen to Khadra. She sat on her plinth, framed by an archway, which, before departing, Abd had not been too rapt to inform me dated from Roman times and had been part of a triple archway built by the Emperor Hadrian. I sat watching Khadra for hours. As dusk beckoned, she ceased to play and, after mingling for a few minutes with the women and children, she joined me, and guided us back to Saida's house.

"Did you miss me?" she asked.

"Yes, I did. I thought I had lost you."

"But you found me."

"With Abd al Bari's help I did. Where did you go?"

"I went yesterday to the Church of the Holy Sepulchre. I found a priest there. I asked him to look at the locket around my neck. I wanted to know if he could tell me about the woman portrayed in it. He told me who it was. It was not my mother. I was sad and cried. I thought I had been wearing my mother's image close to my heart, and that with that image I would be able, eventually, to find her. But it is not to be. My sadness was so great that I could not sing any longer. I handed him my lute to give to another, but he refused it. He said I should keep such a precious instrument, that it should remain my companion. I spent the night in the nearby convent. This morning they wanted me to stay. But I refused. I thought that if I played today, you would come and find me and we could continue the search for my mother."

"But you knew the way to Saida's house. You could have gone there."

"I knew you were not there. I did not know where you were. So, you had to find me. My lute helped you, as it did once before, don't you remember?" She smiled and squeezed my arm.

I looked at her. She had pulled the hood of her abaya closer around her face to hide her tears. I tried to comfort her, hiding my own distress at my abject failure to tell her myself that the image around her neck was not that of her mother.

"What did the priest say to convince you to keep your lute?"

"He said that he had heard me sing, that the lute was my voice and that it could express in music what sometimes I might not be able to say in words." Tears trickled down her cheeks. "I tried to resist his advice. But he insisted I should not despair. He asked me to wait and a short while later he returned with a book."

"What kind of book?"

"A book of lute compositions – ones I have never played before," she replied. "I will show it to you when we reach Saida's house."

We walked on, Khadra's face still half hidden by her hood.

"We will find your mother," I said. "Once we have completed our journey back across the sea, you can relinquish the burden of being a guide to an old man. Then it will be my turn. You, me and your lute – we will find safe haven and you will find your mother and fame."

"I hope that will be so," she murmured.

That evening, we sat in the walled garden. There was little sound, except for Khadra playing on the lute and the fountain. Instead of a gentle Arab melody, she played a fantasia by John Dowland, the notes of which were written in the small battered book that the priest had given her as a keepsake, left behind in the Church of the Holy Sepulchre by some earlier traveller. I had seen it on the table beside her as we ate. It was evident as she followed the pages in the book that Khadra, who I thought only played by ear, already had knowledge of musical notation – yet another mystery I could not fathom. Thus that evening, I, Saida and Bassem, who had now also returned, sat in the garden – our paradise – listening to music that had once been played at the court of Christian IV of Denmark and which now flowed from the lute of a young woman who the day before had been a child.

Three days after we arrived, we left the tranquillity of Saida's house and, again on mules, began our gradual descent from the city towards the coast. As Bassem had promised, the distance was shorter than that we had already travelled, yet it still took us many days to reach the sea. Khadra spoke little and barely touched her lute, except occasionally in the evenings, sitting beside Bassem's nightly fire, the crackling of the twigs a percussive accompaniment to her music, which was now a mix of Arab and Dowland. I did my best to lift her spirits but it was evident no words of mine could console her. From time to time, I would catch her looking at her locket, then burying her face in her hair to avoid revealing her sorrow.

One evening she sang these words from her Dowland book:

> *Flow, my tears, fall from your springs!*
> *Exiled for ever, let me mourn;*
> *Where night's black bird her sad infamy sings,*
> *There let me live forlorn.*

It was all I could do to stop my own tears from flowing.

During the remaining days of our journey we passed a desultory stream of people walking in the opposite direction – old and young, men and women, some cheerful, some looking desolate. Maintaining a steady pace, we sometimes overtook others going in our direction. Every day, as before, we rose early and travelled for hour after hour, pausing only briefly around noon.

One evening, we stopped earlier than usual. For several miles the land we had covered was flat. We entered a village and found a derelict stone structure where once again we ate by a blazing fire.

Bassem broke his silence.

"Tomorrow we will reach the sea. It is but a half-day's walk from here. Once you stand on the shore and I have built you a temporary shelter, my task will be complete." He turned to me. "I have guided you from the sea to the lake far away. I showed you the way to the great city and now I have returned you to the sea across which you came. From dusk tomorrow, it will be you and Khadra alone. I do not know how long you will have to wait for the boatman, but I know he will eventually come to take you back. I cannot say how long your voyage will take. It may be easy, like your voyage to this land, but it may be difficult, perhaps even perilous. Yet with courage and with music you can triumph. When you disembark on the other side, you must lead Khadra to her destiny, whatever it may be. She has faith in you. She is placing her trust in you. Guard her lute, because as she was told in the great city, that is her voice."

"And where will you go, Bassem?"

"I place my life in the hands of another. Like all, I am on the road to the house of the dead. Whether that be near or far I cannot say. It is in the gift of Allah."

His words made me shudder.

It was shortly before noon the following day that we crested the dunes and arrived on the flat sandy shore. I helped Bassem gather wood for a shelter and kindling from amongst the bracken on the ridge's edge. He disappeared for a while, returning with bread, yoghurt, some pieces of lamb, a pot of rice and two extra blankets. He began the fire. We ate in silence, gazing into the crackling flames. The nearby waves lapped quietly. Later, Khadra played the lute softly, and then we slept.

When I awoke, Khadra was at the water's edge looking out across the sea, the rising sun behind her. Bassem was nowhere to be seen. He had gone. We were now alone.

I do not know how long we were on the beach – several days, perhaps. Then one afternoon, as I once more scoured the horizon, I saw a boat in the distance. I watched it come closer. The mast bore a large crimson sail. It seemed similar to the craft that had conveyed us before. As it drew nearer, I saw the boatman dressed in black. Whether he was the same one who had steered our outward voyage, it was hard for me to say, as his face was covered by his keffiyeh. The boat ran onto the sand. Khadra hurried towards it, almost jumping in joy. She darted back towards me.

"It's come," she said. "It's come to take us to your land, the land where I found you. We must board quickly as the boatman will not wait."

She gathered up her lute and blanket and skipped like the child she once was towards the boat. I lingered on the shore, suddenly hesitant about what might lie ahead. Khadra called to me urgently.

"Go and collect your belongings. Quickly. Dusk is falling and we must be gone from here before the night comes. And leave the fire alight, so they know we have left."

"Who are 'they'?"

"I cannot say. But I want them to know I am no longer here."

I collected my blanket, wrapped in it the remaining fruit, picked up the book of Dowland's music Khadra had left on the beach, and boarded the boat. The silent helmsman pushed the craft out until we began to float. Within minutes we were heading swiftly out to sea in the fading daylight.

Khadra drew the hood of her abaya over her head and I put her blanket around her shoulders. Sitting beside me, she turned to me, her face apprehensive.

"You are now my guide. I place my trust in you."

CHAPTER FOUR

Trials

The boat skimmed deftly into dusk and then darkness. Khadra fell asleep, nursed into slumber by the soft sound of the craft's keel caressing the gentle waves. The sail swelled lazily in the soothing breeze. I looked at the boatman, imperturbable and unmoving, the rudder locked beneath his arm. His face shrouded by his keffiyeh, I could not tell whether he was awake or asleep. Gradually, my eyes became heavy and before long I too could not stay awake.

I was woken by a distant keening sound, as though of birds, screeching like gulls do above the furrows left open by the plough. As the boat sailed on in the darkness, the noise became louder, accompanied now by a deep, throbbing vibration. Khadra remained asleep and the boatman showed no reaction, still motionless, his enveloped head sculptured with shadows by the dim lantern swaying on its hook above the stern. Suddenly, the screeching and throbbing stopped. The only sound was once again the gentle waves against the hull. The night was not cold; the wind had a sweet warmth about it. Once more I fell asleep.

I woke as I felt the first focused rays of the morning sun. Khadra had already stirred from her long sleep. Neither of us spoke. The boat continued its journey across a calm, dawn-pink sea rippling in undulant silence all around us. There was no land on the horizon, only infinity. Khadra and I ate some of the fruit I'd brought onboard; I offered it to the boatman but he declined. She and I barely spoke as the morning wore on, preferring the silence surrounding us. Occasionally, a white bird would appear from nowhere and swoop over the deck as though to check our presence, but disappearing as quickly as it had come. Gradually, the wind gathered strength. The crimson sail began to fill to its full extent and we soon increased our speed across the water, now dark blue, the shimmering ripples replaced by more agitated patterns.

Once the sun had passed the midday zenith, the wind suddenly dropped and we were becalmed on a sea of silvered glass. Still the boatman said nothing, still barely moving in his seat. Khadra sat silently, looking out across the mirror-smooth surface, her lute on her lap. It was difficult to say exactly how long we were windless. Perhaps two hours or three had elapsed, judging by the angle of the sun, when we began to pass beneath the edge of a low black cloud of immeasurable proportions that had suddenly appeared in the hitherto cloudless sky. Within minutes, a deep brooding sound started to envelop the boat. The sea quickly turned from silver to blue to dark green then inky black. Rays of the sun penetrated a few cracks in the cloud. But they were extinguished as summarily as they had come, snuffed out by the ever-increasing darkness. Khadra and I peered into the residual light. Spectral, almost formless figures emerged from the water, then slowly sank back into the sea. They uttered no sound. The wind gathered strength once more, sufficient to refill the sail to its full extent, as we travelled on towards the always-darkening horizon, the water becoming more disturbed than ever. Still the boatman barely stirred. Khadra held my hand as fear crossed her face.

A moment later, and in a great howl of wind, an enormous creature leapt from the waves. It stretched a long, scaled arm into the air as though reaching to pluck something from the cloud above. It fell back into the water, only for its head and upper torso to re-emerge seconds later amid shrieks of anger and agony. Its limbs thrashed, causing the waves to become ever rougher, flecked with furious white spume. Once more it sank back, to emerge a third time. Its eyes flashed red, its giant face and green lips tortured by evident pain. It continued to twist and turn in the water, its huge hands almost touching the side of our slender boat. It seemed to cry wordlessly for mercy from some unseen torment. I looked at the boatman, who was fighting hard to control the helm.

As the monster rocked to and fro in the water, its hands now clasped in apparent supplication, Khadra, who had been transfixed by the creature, began to play her lute. Slowly, in manifest response, the dreadful shape ceased its wild movements and began to slide back beneath the surface, just as a passing thunderstorm slips with muted rumbles into the distance. Khadra continued to play. The black cloud started to vanish, the sea once more became blue and the horizon revealed a golden sunset. Again, I turned to the boatman. He was motionless. Looking across the stern, Khadra and I saw that the monster, whatever it was, was following in the boat's wake, its head partially visible, one ear seemingly cocked to the sound of the lute. Minutes before, as the creature writhed in the water, Khadra's music had been frenzied, like a rondo capriccioso, but seeing it docilely following the sound of her instrument, she played a sweet lullaby. Before long the being from the deep finally disappeared.

"He is at peace now," she said, as she continued to play.

Later, in the encroaching gloom, we approached the solitary speck of an island in the now placid sea.

The boatman suddenly spoke.

"I must leave you now. From this point on, you are the arbiters of your own destiny."

I urged him to stay.

"Let him go," said Khadra as she placed a restraining hand on my arm. "This is not a place to dwell. You must now take the helm and steer us on across the sea."

Before I could reply, the boatman stepped from the craft onto the sandy atoll and as he did so, his black keffiyeh slipped to reveal a face slowly transmuting into a skull. I fell back in fright.

"Have no fear," said Khadra. "Quickly, we must go."

The boat, pushed off violently by the deathly figure, picked up a sharp gust of wind which turned us away from the island out to sea. As we gained speed, I gripped the helm tightly, since the craft began seemingly to fly almost of its own accord across the water towards the twilight. Soon it was dark, apart from the glow of the lantern. Khadra played busy, incessant notes on her lute, while the boat sailed on, sometimes fast, sometimes scarcely moving.

That night, we slept little. Khadra played almost without stopping, her music seeming to determine our progress. When dawn broke, still she played, as we seemed to soar across the water. Her face was full of rapturous joy as she stood beneath the mast, her hair flowing in the wind, her black abaya clinging precariously to her slender shoulders, folds billowing as if it were another sail; the rich red of her undergown matched the vivid complexion of the rising sun. Suddenly, she ceased playing and the wind subsided. Within minutes, birds emerged from the water, rising to circle the ship, seeming to echo her music in their calls. Once more, Khadra picked up her lute, responding to their song until together they were in perfect harmony. I sat, my hand on the helm, amazed by the sight and sounds before me. Moments later, the birds disappeared into the distance.

For some hours, we sailed across an almost windless, placid sea beneath a cloudless sky. We talked a little, ate our remaining fruit, and for a while Khadra slept, exhausted by her musical exertions. I continued at the helm, making sure the wind was behind me. From where the sun was slowly beginning its descent, I calculated that the boat was taking us in a north-easterly direction. My eyes raked the horizon for land. Then, as if out of nowhere, I observed two ships coming towards us. As they approached, the smaller of the two – though still more than twice the size of our craft – began to circle us, coming ever closer. I counted at least four onboard. They were dishevelled, rough-looking individuals armed with long knives and dressed in a combination of Arab dress and pantaloons. They could only be pirates.

"Heave to," came the cry. "Show us what you are carrying."

I sailed on, aiming to take advantage of a sudden strengthening wind to squeeze between the two vessels. A shot rang out. Khadra woke, fear freezing her face as she saw a thick-bearded pirate reach out with a grappling hook to snare our boat. Unsure of what to do, I wrenched the helm and we escaped the hook, the pirate falling into the water. Another shot was fired, this time from the larger ship, now close to us as well. As the smaller ship again came alongside, one of its crew leapt onto our boat. A rope flung after him landed on our deck, and the invader used it to secure our craft to his.

"Now, let's see what you've got for us." He bent down beneath the prow of the ship to peer into the small open compartment where Khadra sometimes slept. He called out to his companions that there was nothing. Khadra clung to my side.

"We'll kill him and take her to the market," he shouted to the crew of the larger ship now bearing down on us. "She'll fetch a fine price."

He pulled a short length of cord from his pocket and lunged at Khadra, clearly intending to tie her wrists.

In an instant, the sky went dark and the sea frothed wildly. The rope securing us to the smaller vessel broke and, seeking to retrieve it, the pirate fell, tumbling and screaming, into the foam. Suddenly, the monster we had encountered earlier hurtled from the water and with one giant hand dragged the smaller ship down into the deep. Immediately returning to the surface, it reached higher into the sky and grasped part of the rigging of the larger ship. The crew surged forward in terror, trying to release the monster's grip. But as they neared it with knives, swords and cutlasses drawn, it spat out a great jet of inky black water, sending them sprawling. With a hurricane howl of rage, it hauled on the rigging and in a second had broken the rear mast. The creature rocked the boat to and fro, harder and harder until it capsized, sending the remaining pirates scattering into the sea. Two clung to the side of our boat, trying to climb aboard, but the monster broke their grip and thrust them kicking under the water. Finally, with one last howl of fury, it pushed the upturned hull deep beneath the waves. It was a miracle that our boat did not sink in the suction of the frenzied whirlpool.

Within minutes, the struggle was over. The two ships had vanished. All that was left on the surface were some broken spars of wood and a red keffiyeh. The monster rested its vast body on the water for a few seconds and then, looking at Khadra as it did so, began to disappear. Khadra picked up her lute and played – first, frantic music and then a quieter, more soothing melody. The creature slowly rose once more into view and seemed to bow to

Khadra, before sliding for the last time beneath the placid surface of the sea.

It was some time before Khadra and I regained our composure. The breeze quickened once again, twilight came and then darkness. Though the wind was moderate, it became cooler and we wrapped our blankets around us as we ate the remaining morsels of food. A look of hopelessness passed across her face; I sought to reassure her.

"I do not know where our voyage will lead, or how much longer it will take, but I sense it may end soon, and in safety. Have faith, Khadra. I will protect you as long as there is a breath in my body."

She smiled. "I know you will. I too sense our journey will end soon, whether we will be saved or die."

Keeping as warm as we could in the chilling breeze, we sailed on in silence. Khadra played her lute for a while before falling asleep. I sat awake, my hand on the tiller, aware that behind me there remained a trail of froth in the water. I could only imagine that the creature was keeping guard over the musician who eased its pain, the legacy of whatever fate had befallen it in the past.

Before dawn, the wind dropped once more. In the early hours of the new day, while Khadra still slept, our boat became enveloped in a warm, thickening mist. There was no sound, save that of the water whispering against the hull. It was hard to say how long we were wrapped in this fog. Then, the sun began to penetrate and in minutes the mist rolled back. Khadra stirred. As the last shreds of sea haze evaporated in the sun's increasing heat, I saw in the distance, to the left and to the right, the faint outline of land. Khadra clapped her hands in joy.

"Bravo! We are nearly there. We are in sight of land. Surely, the shores of Europe – my new home. We have overcome the forces of darkness, conquered our self-doubt. Now, I can begin my life in earnest. But do not leave me, Mr Helmsman. Stay with me. You are familiar with this world while I am not."

She sat in the prow, the music of her lute matching the pulse of the boat as it bucked against each breasting wave. Once more we gathered speed, once more soaring across the water. Soon, to either side, gigantic ships and galleys passed us, heading in the direction we had come. Then, after a while, we saw the shadowy silhouette of a city. Khadra played on, her fingers flying across the strings of the lute, as before the boat seeming to respond to the frenzy of her music. I looked behind us and saw the long plume of foam-flecked water; perhaps the monster was still there, propelling us forward to our destination.

Our pace slowing, we sailed close enough to a small island on our right to hear the multitude of birds singing in its trees. Khadra turned and played a gentle but insistent tune on her instrument as though to accompany them. We approached another island to our left. The birdsong from the trees became incessant, as if greeting the lute player. Soon, a much larger island came into view. The wind dropped to a gentle breeze, the boat slowed further and the spume behind us disappeared. We glided past moored boats – large and small, some simple, some richly decorated – and drew alongside a bank of lush grass with a flourish of trees and flowers at the top. Khadra stepped ashore. The chorus of birds became deafening. She cast aside her abaya and danced in circles beneath the trees, her arms outstretched. The hum of bees seemed to join the symphony of sound.

A small boat came up beside me. I asked the occupant where we were. He looked at me in astonishment.

"My friend, do you not know? Further along, at the far end of this lagoon, is the Grand Canal, the Doge's Palace, the great cathedral of St Mark. Sir, you are in the great city of Venice, La Serenissima."

I thanked him.

"Where have you come from?" he asked.

"From the south and the east beyond," I replied.

"And who is she, the one who seems so joyous?" He pointed to Khadra.

"She is an incomparable player of the lute. She was shipwrecked as a child. Though now a young woman, she still searches for her long-lost mother."

"Was it her who was playing as you passed the island over there? I was behind you and heard her music carried on the wind."

"Yes, it was her."

"There is a place in this city in search of fine lute players – indeed, fine musicians of every instrument."

"Which place is that?"

"The Ospedale della Pietà. It's a place for orphans, for those whose families cannot support them. It has a well-known musical ensemble, all young ladies. There is a priest there – a talented musician and composer. You should take her there and seek an audience with him."

"Thank you. Perhaps we will go. But it will be her decision, not mine. What is the man's name?" I asked.

"Signor Antonio Vivaldi," he replied.

CHAPTER FIVE

The Temptation of La Serenissima

The day after our arrival in Venice, we made our way to the Ospedale. We entered the great hall, where presided a man in a frock coat, his hair distinctively red. Around him sat musicians and above, in the gallery, was a choir of women. Khadra and I stood in amazement as the music flowed in waves around us.

"What are they singing?" I asked a man standing close to us.

"It's the *Gloria*, one of his compositions," he said, gesturing towards the man in the frock coat.

Khadra remained motionless, as though in a trance, as we listened to the *Agnus Dei*. When the music ended, the composer, Signor Vivaldi, rose to acknowledge the orchestra and choir. He turned and walked towards us. As he approached, Khadra curtsied.

"And who are you, young woman?" he asked.

"I am Khadra, a lute player."

"Is that the case, young lady? I am always seeking lute players."

"She plays well," I interjected.

"Let me, sir, be the judge of that. Come back tomorrow."

"If it please you, may I play to you now?" Khadra ventured.

He looked at her and then snapped his fingers. "Bring her a lute. Let us see how good she is."

"There is no need for that, sir. She has her own lute." I picked up the instrument on the chair behind me. He examined it but said nothing.

"Come with me," he instructed Khadra, as he headed towards a red-velvet chair and a stool beside it. He held out some sheets of music. "Can you read music?"

"Not that well. But I can remember music. I can repeat what I hear."

"I see. Let me play and then you repeat it."

He sat beside her and played her lute without looking at the sheets of music, now scattered on the floor around him.

"Now it's your turn." He handed her the lute. "I see that it was made in France," he commented.

Khadra did not acknowledge his observation. After a pause, she began to play. I watched the composer's face, looking at her intently as she played with great skill and tenderness, repeating note for note what she had heard. I recalled the first time I had seen her – a child then – in the cathedral, summoning me towards the boat that had taken us to a distant shore. Signor Vivaldi continued to gaze at her, evidently struck by her grace and ability. He let her perform until the end of the largo he had played to her.

When she finished, he sat without speaking. Then he stood.

"At last, you have come. I have waited so long for this moment – to find a supremely talented lutenist. I invite you to join my musicians."

Khadra appeared to hesitate.

"Signorina Khadra, I urge you. Please join us and stay."

She nodded.

Within weeks, word of Khadra's musical virtuosity – and her striking features – had spread and she became the talk of the city, to which I can attest as a first-hand witness of her growing fame. Since all were of the opinion that I, poorly dressed and without financial means, was unable to provide for her, I was prevailed upon to agree to her admission to the *seminario musicale* of the Ospedale della Pietà on the Riva degli Schiavoni near the Ponte del Sepolcro. Signor Vivaldi was its acknowledged luminary.

Established originally as a charitable institution intended to care for foundlings and orphans, its fame now rested on its reputation as a school for the teaching of music, highlighted by the city-wide renown of Vivaldi – teacher, orchestra maestro, composer, violinist and purchaser of instruments, all without obvious detriment to his well-publicised role of theatrical musician and impresario. Khadra was reluctant to be parted from me, as indeed I was from her, since each of us viewed the other as an inseparable companion. But neither she nor I could resist the composer's persuasion. She was immediately appointed a musician – a *figlie del coro* – earning the *seminario* a hundred lire or so towards her upkeep (the school and orchestra had no shortage of wealthy patrons in a city flush with money and where women were a lucrative commodity). But in a matter of weeks her skill on the lute had led to her joining the *seminario*'s elite *privilegiate del coro*, thus, I was told, opening the way to acts of homage, gifts and proposals of marriage.

Before three months passed she had become lionised – a beautiful, young, flawless lutenist, often besieged by reverent young admirers and lecherous older men as she performed in magnificent palazzi along the main canal, in the cathedral and churches. Not long after, Khadra informed me that she had been baptised into the Catholic faith and given the name of Cecilia, in honour of the patron saint of music. I regretted the disappearance of Khadra but she and I agreed that in private I could still call her by that name.

The orphanage administrators had found me pleasant if rather bare rooms on the first floor of a nearby small, somewhat dilapidated palazzo, halfway along a side canal whose water often gave off a pungent, unpleasant odour that lessened only when it rained. I appeared to be the only occupant of the palazzo, apart from a large, imposing bronze figure of the Emperor Vespasian at the top of the main staircase, his expression displaying profound bad temper at being so cruelly neglected. They kindly gave me fresh clothes also. I frequently walked to get fresher air and sometimes, with the money Khadra generously shared with me – a small amount, for her earnings in those early days were modest – I bought a book or two to read in the long evenings alone. A high day would be one on which I received a letter from her, explaining her absence from promised time together and giving me her latest news. I enjoyed receiving them, not just for their contents but for the patience required to read them – her handwriting was more akin to Arabic script. The sentiments she expressed were full of excitement, sometimes naively childlike. I kept each letter in a leather pouch I had found on a market stall.

Most evenings, I ate alone in what once would have been a magnificent library, judging by the empty, dusty shelves. Food, some wine and fresh candles were brought to my rooms on the first floor by an aged woman whose name I was never able to discover but who after a while I decided to call Maddalena, the name inscribed in a book of poetry I had bought. She appeared mysteriously three times a day, never speaking, always turning her head away if I sought to pass the time of day. I could only assume that the food she provided also came courtesy of the *seminario*. When I went to bed, I often lay awake, speculating as to who she might be, what she might have looked like when younger – and, of course, how I came to be where I was.

As summer turned to autumn, Khadra's fame became even greater. Consequently, we saw each other less and less, except when I went to one of her concerts. To while away the time, I walked for ever longer periods each day, returning to my rooms to record some of the sights and sounds of the city in a commonplace book I had bought, and to piece together fragments of its history, reflected in the buildings I observed. One afternoon, I sensed I was being followed. I would turn to look but no one was there. Several days later, I again believed there was someone close behind, watching me, but each time I stopped to see who in the crowd it might be, there was no sign of a pursuer. This sense of being watched began to unnerve me. I told Khadra about it on one of the rare occasions she was free to join me for supper. She smiled and told me I was surely mistaken.

One evening a week later I was reading before going to bed. The old woman had cleared away my plate and before nodding goodnight – a new development on her part – poured me another glass of wine. She shut the door behind her and, seated beside the fire she had lit for me earlier, I heard the sound of her light, uneven footsteps disappear down the long, winding wooden staircase. As sometimes happened I fell asleep in my chair but woke after a while at the noise of the book falling on the floor. I stooped to pick it up.

The fire had subsided and I placed several more pieces of wood on the much-diminished flames. As I did so, I heard the staircase creak. I thought it might be Maddalena returning with more wine, but as the steps grew closer, I detected a heavier, more deliberate tread. There was a pause. I called out.

"Who's there?"

I was about to stir from my seat to go to the door when it opened. A figure entered, a man, I judged, from the build visible in the candlelight. He came towards me out of the shadow.

"Please, do not get up. Let me join you by the fire."

He sat down opposite me. He wore a long blue gown, opened at the front revealing a pale-pink lining, white stockings, blue breeches, a reddish-pink jacket and red shoes; his cuffs were elegant lace. He had on the customary short grey wig, but his face was concealed by a mask – a mask that seemed fixed in its own smile, unless perhaps it was reflecting the smile on the face behind it.

"Who are you? Why do you come uninvited at such a late hour?"

"Do not be afraid. I have come to make conversation."

"About what?"

"About life," the mask replied.

"Philosophers since ancient times have discoursed at length about life. As for me, I am no philosopher. Just an ordinary mortal of advancing years. Moreover, it is too late to debate."

"A lame excuse. Come, you can do better than that!"

"It is now approaching midnight," I replied irritably. "I am fatigued, and it is the valid truth, not an excuse, that I did not ask you – whoever you are – to come and debate such a subject at this late hour. I suggest you leave."

"Are you man or animal?"

My irritation grew – along with uncertainty. I did not know whether the conversation in which I was being encouraged to participate was real or imagined. Was this the beginning of another perilous voyage taking me to a destination even further removed from where I wished to return, that place from which I had set out in pursuit of a distant melody carried on the wind? Becoming increasingly concerned I had been consigned to a limbo with any help beyond my reach, I had no wish, as the nearby church bell struck midnight, to take a further step into the unknown. I therefore declined to answer his question.

"Come, I asked you. Are you man or animal?" he repeated.

Trying to suppress my mounting anger, I replied, "I am not an animal but a man."

"What is the reason for your answer?"

He had hooked me. I thought hard about how I should reply.

"Was it not Descartes who said in his treatise, 'cogito, ergo sum' – 'I think, therefore I am'? Given that premise, you and I think, animals do not."

"But Descartes said more than that."

"I know he did. But what I believe he meant by that remark was that, whether God exists or not, it is impossible for man to doubt that he himself exists, for to doubt he must first exist, else he would not be able to doubt."

The mask's smile seemed to widen.

"There. Despite the late hour, you have the knowledge of a philosopher. But I must persist. What makes you conclude you are not an animal?"

"When will you cease asking questions?"

"Only when I have a satisfactory answer!"

"I can only answer in the way I know and understand."

"And what is that way?"

"Compared to an animal of any description, man is the most sophisticated form of life. We think, we decide and we live what we decide."

"Can you prove that?"

My impatience at my inquisitor's persistence was now barely controlled.

"It can be said man demonstrates three aspects of life. Physical, our bodily existence. The working of our minds, with which we think – our curiosity to acquire knowledge. And our spirit."

"What do you mean by 'spirit'?"

"That is hard to explain, but perhaps the best definition is that it is our conscience, our awareness of what is right or wrong – if we choose to be aware of it. On the other hand, we may choose to ignore our conscience."

"And what of *your* conscience? What part has it played in your life?"

"That is a private matter."

"Why do you say that? Do you have something to hide, either from me or from yourself?"

A wave of anguish overcame me. I was nearing a door I had kept securely locked for years.

"Come, Johannes, hide nothing."

"How do you know my name?"

"I know these things. I ask again, what have you tried to hide from in your life? You can tell me."

"You are not my confessor!"

"No, I am not your confessor. You could say I am your conscience, perhaps. Why not reveal what has long been concealed in the depth of your mind?"

I struggled with anger, resentment and guilt as I looked at the masked man, the flames of the fire reflected on his hideously smiling countenance. Suddenly, I could not hold my secret any more.

"I was once cruel – in my ambition, in my selfishness and in my rejection of love towards me. I realised afterwards what a fool I had been, how callous. But the realisation came too late. I had lost what I should have treasured, never to find it again."

I buried my face in my hands. When I looked up, the chair the figure had occupied was empty. I opened the door to see if it might be descending the stairs, but there was nothing, just darkness. I sat before the fire well into the night, watching the wood burn, unnerved by my unwelcome interlocutor and discomfited by the memories he had elicited. I must then have fallen asleep. I woke, bathed in a shaft of sunlight. My breakfast was upon the table.

I tried hard in the ensuing days to forget the masked man, reasoning that it must have been a dream and that in due course even the most disturbing dreams can be forgotten or at least pushed aside by pressing preoccupations and other recollections. I walked as often and as briskly as I could. Each afternoon I took to the water, befriended by an old gondolier, Giuseppe, who told me stories of past times on the canals. It was hard to follow all he said, his words, to my untuned ear, sometimes a babbling brook of incoherence. On such occasions I just smiled and nodded my head, enjoying his company none the less. Some evenings I would go to the *seminario* to hear music, my regular attendance rewarded by a reserved chair. As my purse mysteriously never emptied, I acquired more books, including one on human anatomy and another on the human condition, both of which took their place on the empty bookshelves of my favourite room. But in my more solitary moments I could not rid from my mind the image of the man with the smiling mask.

In Venice, music was everywhere – in the cathedral, churches, the grand palaces and in other *istituti* for foundlings and the orphaned. The music I heard, whether resounding in a palazzo or wafting through the narrow streets and across the water, was often sublime. One evening, at a performance in the Doge's Palace, Khadra appeared with a young violinist to play a medley of galliards and other musical fripperies. Seated beneath striking portraits of biblical figures – one of the largest being Salome, averting her gaze from the head of John the Baptist – she wore an off-the-shoulder décolleté crimson velvet dress, edged in gold-encrusted braid, her long hair pinned up, accentuating its varied shades, and held in place with two jewelled ornamental combs. She settled herself on the high-backed damask-covered chair, her left foot on a silver stool, cradling a theorbo, an instrument I had not seen her play before, then began the recital with deep concentration,. Once, she looked up and caught sight of me in the corner. She smiled. Later, I saw her smile at a handsome, finely dressed young man, sitting in the front row alongside several bejewelled male companions.

Upon returning to my lodgings through the nightly mist rising from the canal, I found Maddalena setting the supper table for two.

"No, there is no need for that. Signorina Khadra is not coming this evening."

She looked at me questioningly, and, despite my insistence that I would be eating alone, completed her task. Shortly, she returned with wine and a simple array of meats, cheeses and fruit, nodding her satisfaction at the inviting result. I suddenly noticed that she was attired differently from her normal shabby, monochrome dress and shawl; her bonnet was different too. Over a white, puff-sleeved chemise gathered tightly at the ribs by a wide blue ribbon, she wore a long, front-buttoning orange gown, cinched at the waist, from whose elbow-length sleeves billowed the muslin of the chemise beneath. Her bonnet, also white, was close-fitting and tied neatly under her chin. What's more, at her side, almost concealed by her skirts, was a young boy, aged perhaps three or four, dressed in an ankle-length red robe, white trim around the collar and with silver embroidery on the cuffs and down the centre. I had never seen the child before. Like Maddalena, he did not speak, never letting go of her skirts, to which he clung doggedly. I went to greet him but he hid ever deeper in the folds of the dress, a look of acute apprehension on his face. With the food laid on the table and the candles lit, Maddalena and the boy left.

Not yet ready to eat and mystified by the setting for two, Maddalena's change of clothes and the appearance of the boy, I sat by the fire. The clock had just struck ten when I heard the heavy tread of footsteps approaching the door. I knew who it would be. There was a gentle knock and then the figure entered, dressed as before.

"Thank you for your kind and generous invitation to supper. I saw you return from the palace – later than I had expected, so I waited a while for Maddalena to prepare before arriving. Shall we sit at the table and eat? After all, that is why I am here."

My unavoidable guest had arrived. I motioned for him to take his place.

"How did you know she is called Maddalena? That is the name I gave her at random as she would not tell me what it really is."

"She cannot speak – mute since childhood. And how did I know she is called Maddalena? I knew because that is indeed her name. You, not knowing that, chose it for her because it was inscribed in a book of poetry you bought. That book once belonged to her, but it was stolen, along with other items, by unscrupulous scoundrels following the death of her beloved husband. She is happy that the book now rests in this room in your possession. Now, shall we eat?"

I gestured to him to begin, even as I struggled to take in the coincidence of the book being Maddalena's.

"Who are you?" I asked. "And who invited you, since I did not?"

"My friend, I choose my eating companions with care. Often, they are alone, lost in limbo. Have you not felt yourself to be thus isolated and adrift?"

"I'm not yet dead, so I would like to think I am not yet in limbo – that space where, I was once told by a priest, it is decided who should descend into the pits of damnation and who should take the first steps towards salvation."

"I agree you are not yet in that limbo but you are aimless, just like the boat that was sometimes becalmed on your voyage to Venice from across the sea." He laughed. "I can see the question on your lips. How did I know you were becalmed? I know because you talk in your sleep. You have written about it in your commonplace book. And sometimes when you and the young woman meet you recall the voyage."

"How do you know all this? You must spy on us," I accused.

"I don't spy. I observe. I am in your mind. I'm your conscience, your recollection of times past, time wasted, opportunities missed."

Our conversation lasted beyond midnight, ebbing and rising like the proverbial tide.

As the clock struck one, he posed a further question.

"What are you going to do with the rest of your life? Stay here – be a mere bystander, a passive spectator of the passage of time? Or has the hour come for you to participate with energy, conviction and joy in what remains of your life? You have been in this city for many weeks. Surely, you must be close to deciding what to do?"

"I have not yet decided, except in one regard."

"And what is that?" the smiling mask asked.

"The young woman, Khadra, lured me with her music to board a boat that took me to a distant land. From there, she and I sailed to this city, protected by a creature of the deep."

"That was me," he interjected. "I take many forms. Her music soothed my anguish and I repaid that gift by guiding you here, protecting you from evil doers and spirits."

I was lost for words, spilling my wine in shock. It was the reappearance of a nightmare.

"I want to return to where I came from. That is all," I mumbled.

"Are you staying because you have fallen in love with Khadra?"

"No. I vow that is not the case and never shall be. I admire her, I enjoy her companionship, and her music bewitches me. But without her I don't know the way back. I can only wait patiently for the time when I can persuade her to resume our journey to the north."

"Are you not deceiving yourself? Did I not observe envy, perhaps even jealousy, when you saw her smile at the young man in the palace, a look possibly concealing a promise of carnal pleasure? Did I not detect a wish that she would give you such a knowing smile?"

"No, no, no. You are mistaken. She is like a daughter, not a woman for sexual enjoyment."

"Let me reveal the truth. Khadra is acclaimed as a lutenist. But she is equally worshipped for her body. For those with money to spend, she is the perfect combination – an accomplished musician endowed with great beauty. Her head is already being turned by wealth, by adulation. She will not leave here, my friend. Before the next winter is over she will be an illustrious courtesan. And you will be forgotten."

"That is not true. She has promised me we will leave here for the north."

The mask seemed to smile an even broader smile.

"That may never happen. Why wait in daily isolation for a journey that may never come to pass? Give her up. Let her be free to do as she wishes – and then to assuage her guilt, if indeed she should feel any, at leaving you on an unfinished journey. You can ease the pain of parting from her, by spending time with the courtesans here. It will be so easy, so painless, so enjoyable."

"No. Never. I will never do so. I will wait until Khadra is ready. She will not desert me. Together, we will go north."

"I wager you will not, that you will lose, that I will win the argument."

"Whoever you are, conscience as you say or satanic tempter as you seem, you will not prevail. She will leave Venice and together we will retrace our steps."

"So be it," the mask replied. "Let the best man win."

For many days after that exchange I was afflicted by dreams, even in daytime full of unease, as though once again I were standing on the edge of a precipice. I saw little of Khadra, often ignoring opportunities to see her perform but belatedly realising that if I continued to avoid her, it could be construed as a manifestation of the jealousy of which the masked man had accused me. I resolved to return to the Palazzo Ducale, where she was due to be playing.

The concert was on Ascension Day. Earlier, the Doge, accompanied by the nobility and the senate, had sailed out into the lagoon in a special golden barge to toss into the water a ceremonial ring symbolising the city's marriage to, and indeed its domination of, the sea. The grand gallery, illuminated by myriads of candles, quickly filled. In the front sat the rich, the famous, the powerful and the aspirants to greatness, together with Venetian patricians dressed in long black gowns, mingling with nobles from other parts of Europe. Amongst them, on his throne, sat the Doge in his finery, the perceived earthly link between the city – founded centuries before on the Feast of the Annunciation and designated a Christian realm built from the ruins of ancient Rome – the sea on which its fortunes had flourished and, ultimately, the Virgin, the city's patron, and the goddess Venus. I sat on a stool, high above the gallery, observing this tableau of pageantry and wealth.

The orchestra entered, in their midst Khadra, wearing a gown of golden taffeta and carrying the lute I had heard her play so often. I was transfixed by her beauty, by her transformation from the young girl who had played to me in Palestine to a tall, elegant, beautiful woman, who could easily captivate anyone, male or female. Perhaps the smiling mask was right – that I had indeed fallen in love with her, that he would win his wager.

After the concert, I was pressed to join others in the continuing celebration of the day. I drank deep into the night. Many congratulated me on bringing such a fine musician to the city, and of such beauty too. I saw Khadra in the distance, surrounded by young admirers urging her to play for them on her lute – they flirting with her and she responding in kind. I was approached by a stylish woman in a rich-blue décolleté velvet gown. She took my hand.

"You must be sad to lose the affection of that young woman."

"I'm not sad. I'm pleased she has found fame and happiness in this city. I wish her well. Besides, I believe it is not her affection that has been lost, merely the time in which to show it. I hope one day she and I might still travel north, as we planned, so others can hear her music."

"Johannes, you may have to wait quite a while, judging by her conduct this evening. Perhaps you and I might spend time together instead. I would like to hear more of your adventures from before your arrival in the city. Come, another drink."

We talked until the small hours and eventually left the palace together, riding *à deux* in her private gondola towards her palazzo.

"You must see the dawn rise across the lagoon from my window."

"Signora, I cannot. It would be improper for me to do so."

"Signore, there is no charge for what I propose. You and I are older than others. Let us simply enjoy each other's company."

We arrived at her luxurious palazzo, which was full of ornate wall hangings and pictures and much silver plate. Her staff greeted her with deference as she and I went upstairs to a sumptuous bedroom with a large window facing the lagoon. She gave me a goblet of wine. Before long she kissed me and shortly thereafter I was in her bed. After watching the sun rise, I returned to my humble lodgings, ashamed of what I had done, my anguish all the greater for the words she had spoken as I left.

"So, Johannes, shall we meet again and thus finally break Khadra's spell? There is much we can achieve together. I will expect you tonight."

I sat alone and wept. Had the man in the smiling mask already won his wager?

Almost a week later, Maddalena brought me a message. It was from Khadra. She wished to talk to me urgently.

Wearing a plush grey cloak over the crimson gown I had seen her in before, at the Doge's Palace, she was pale, her eyes tearful. We embraced and sat together in front of the fire, her lute beside her as always. I waited for her to speak.

"I wish to leave Venice immediately – to go north, with you as my companion."

"Why do you wish to leave, when the whole city is at your feet?"

"I cannot stay. This city is not for me. If I stay, I will be unhappy."

"What has caused you to think this?"

She hesitated for the slightest of moments before answering.

"A nobleman, Octaviano, befriended me – enchanted by my music, he claimed. I enjoyed his charm and his gifts of adulation, as he called them. He introduced me to others in his circle and we dined together. Then, one evening, he said he had fallen in love with me and wished to marry me, but that as a young man from a most distinguished and wealthy family, he could not offer his hand until his father died. He proposed that, until that time came, I be his lover, as was his heartfelt desire. Night after night he pressed his case, until I succumbed and we slept together. In the days that followed, he presented me with gorgeous clothes and made me wear *zoccoli*, as he said they gave me greater height and presence. The gowns he ordered to be made for me were refined, sophisticated, with chains of gold and orient pearls. My head was turned. I longed for him to touch me, to hold me. My music became of less importance.

"Then a week ago I encountered a young woman, Nezetta, whose friendship I had enjoyed in my first days at the *seminario*. When she saw me, she laughed. I asked her why. She said I was dressed like a courtesan, that the young man who had pledged his love was treating me as a prostitute, providing me with fine clothes to demonstrate his dominance over me. We talked long into the night. The next day, at the *seminario*, I heard her sing exquisitely. Signor Vivaldi asked me to play a new piece he had composed. To my dismay he said my music had lost its lustre.

"That evening I confronted Octaviano. He urged me once more into his bed, in order to remove silly thoughts from my head. But I was so distressed I could not give him what he desired. He became brutish and the next day he came to see me at my lodgings – where I have been staying at my own expense, not his, with money earned from my performances. He insisted that I return the clothes he had given me so he could be refunded their unnecessary cost. I lost my temper and threw him out. But he and a masked man have been following me, intent I am certain on either destroying my reputation as a musician or prevailing upon me to relent. I will not." Tears spilled from her eyes. "I am so sorry, Johannes. I have neglected you, cast you aside, despite all your kindness. That was unforgivable. I beg your forgiveness nevertheless. Will you once again let me be your companion, so that we can leave this city together and travel north?"

"There is nothing to forgive," I replied. "What you have experienced is the way of the world – full of cruelty and deception. Put the experience behind you. Put your music first. In the morning, we will leave."

That night Khadra stayed at the palazzo with me. She took my bed, while I slept in the chair in front of the fire in the library.

I woke in the middle of the night, chilled, as the fire had subsided. I banked it with fresh logs and, after checking Khadra was safe in the bedroom, I sat once more before the hearth and fell asleep. Whether still slumbering or awake, I was led by Maddalena onto a balcony beyond which was the boundless universe, just as I had seen it in the cathedral before commencing my journey across the sea with Khadra. But instead of darkness illuminated by stars, this time the heavens were a swirling mass of brilliant, burning colours bursting silently into fountains of liquid violence, blazing across the whole celestial panorama before me. There was no sound, save the gentle whistle of a distant wind.

I heard a voice behind me.

"You have not won the wager yet, Johannes. There is still far to go before I concede defeat. Take her with you to the north. But I will follow. You may be sure of that." His words ended with the echo of laughter that seemed to fill the universe beyond the balcony.

Stepping back from the window I expected to see the man in the smiling mask, but he was not there. Instead, before me, in the middle of the room, were twelve dancers, resplendent and sinister in carnival costume – a Pantalone, Columbina, *medico della peste*, a cat – whirling to frenzied music played by Khadra on her lute, her face revelling in the marvel of the masqueraders she had conjured from the dark corners of the room. Beside her was a tiny elf, playing the flute with similar passion. As the tempo increased, so the dancers spun ever faster until they converged in a flash of coruscating light that revealed a long winding road. The elf, frenetically playing his flute, began to dance an Irish jig. Khadra joined in on her lute.

"Come, Johannes, we must follow him. He's showing us the way – to the north."

"Let me gather my books. I must take my books."

"There's no time for books. Maddalena will care for them. We must leave now. Come, we must go."

"But how will we go?"

"We will go by elephant! Just as Hannibal once did, over the mountains!" said Khadra with peals of laughter.

I followed her, the elf dancing ahead playing an even more feverish melody, matched by Khadra on the lute. Then I saw the elephant – white, the wrinkles of its skin veined in gold, its back covered by a richly embroidered dark-blue cloth with a grinning gorgon's face on each side, and a crown on its head. A rope ladder unfolded from its shoulder. The pixie quickly climbed it, then Khadra, and finally me. As the elephant began to move, swaying from side to side in the darkness, a child's voice called out.

"Please, don't leave me behind."

I peered down to see the little boy who had hidden in Maddalena's skirts. He tried to grasp the end of the rope ladder.

Maddalena scurried beside him, urging us silently with outstretched arms to take him. We stopped. I descended the ladder and, reaching out for the boy's hand, gradually pulled him up. He sat beside me as the elephant lumbered forward, the pixie dancing another jig in the centre of the crown on its head, Khadra accompanying him on her lute. And so we swayed into the night.

As dawn broke, we were already in the foothills of the mountains, towering peaks covered in snow ahead of us. I looked back. The city of Venice had disappeared from view but in the middle distance I could see a petrel dipping and rising. It never came closer but hour after hour maintained its position as though watching our progress. I could only guess it was the man in the smiling mask in a new form, honouring his promise to dog our steps.

CHAPTER SIX

The Forest

Though I resisted sleep as best I could for fear of falling from my precarious perch on the elephant's back, without any accurate means to tell the time of day, I cannot say with any exactitude how many hours passed before we neared the end of our trek over the mountains. Throughout our journey it was neither day nor night but a perpetual half-light of changing hues – a kaleidoscope of rainbow colours. The snow was deep and in places seemingly impassable but the stately animal, to which Khadra gave the name Khan, maintained a steady and relentless pace. The elf played his flute, rarely stopping to take a breath. The boy said nothing, tightly gripping Khadra, who sat in front of me, her lute in its familiar position across her back. Though the wind blew constantly, sweeping snow from one side of our path to higher ground on our right, we were not cold despite our lack of suitable clothing for such terrain. It was as if we were cocooned in an invisible pocket of warmth.

Suddenly, the half-light vanished, as though the curtains concealing a vast stage had been swept back, to reveal a scene of unprecedented wonder. Khan was wending his way along a high, narrow ridge. To our left was a sharply falling escarpment, with its lower reaches shrouded in billowing cloud, while to our right, far below, were the peaks of snow-covered mountains. Ahead, the sky was a dazzling mix of different shades of blue streaked with countless meteors, each with a fiery orange tail. Some distance further on, the ridge along which the elephant was treading with increasing care appeared to fork: to the left, downwards towards the cloud-filled valley and to the right, in the direction of endless folds of mighty mountains. As we approached the point of decision, Khadra began to play her lute, accompanied sweetly by the elf on his flute, as though giving Khan inspiration for the choice he would have to make. She had scarcely begun to pluck the strings when Khan abruptly stopped. After swinging his head from left to right several times, he gave a prodigious roar and, at the fork in the path, turned to the left to descend a narrow trail down towards the shrouded valley below.

As we crossed the snow line, the azure-blue sky gradually dulled to a deep sullen grey. With Khan's back at an ever-steeper angle, so leaving us clutching fiercely the fabric on which we sat, we slowly approached a ledge directly overlooking the mist-filled void below, with only the tops of trees eerily piercing the vaporous veil. Khan paused, gave another roar and after stamping the ground several times continued his descent to the gentle sound of the soothing lute and the playful flute. We soon became enveloped in thick, clinging mist, quickly losing all sense of our surroundings, knowing only, from our battle with balance and gravity, that we were still on a downward path, which was becoming less and less uneven as the elephant took each step. Then in the blink of an eye the mist vanished and we found ourselves in a forest. Khan stopped and knelt to allow us to descend.

I stood on the forest floor, which was densely strewn with crisp, autumn-burnished leaves, grateful for its flatness and stability.

"Journey's end," said the elf in his squeaky voice. The elephant snorted as though in agreement after his hours of exertion.

I looked around. Judging by the height of the trees and the girth of their creviced trunks, it was an ancient forest, the floor snaked with gnarled, sinewy roots. Ahead, through clumps of trees stretching into the far distance, I caught glimpses of the sky – purple streaked with orange and yellow. To our right was a stream trickling through the fallen leaves. Beyond that stood two horses, harnessed between the shafts of a cart, seemingly abandoned. There was no sign of human habitation. It was a place of apparent desolation.

The silence was disturbed by rustling and creaking behind us.

Turning, I saw Khan rear up on his hind legs and begin to sprout branches. His upright body quickly become the trunk of a huge tree. His soulful eyes were the last feature to disappear, becoming lifeless rings, the knotted scars of long-perished branches. The elf sat on a bough in the tree's crown. With a final trill on his flute, he changed into an owl looking down at us, one eye closed, the other doubly penetrating in its stare. The flute was tucked beneath its wing.

We were now alone in the forest, without direction or comfort. The boy gripped Khadra's hand, his face full of fear.

"Which way should we go?" she asked.

I felt keenly the responsibility now resting on my shoulders – Khadra and her search for her mother, and the boy without a name who had spoken no further words since imploring us not to leave him behind in Venice. I looked at the sluggish trickle of water.

"We should follow the flow of the stream. It could lead us to a village, a town, perhaps even to the coast, since most streams join rivers and rivers end in the sea."

Khadra nodded in agreement. And so we began to walk, closely following the stream. The sky remained unchanging in its streaked purple colour but the density of the forest varied, sometimes an abundance of trees with the canopy so interwoven it was impossible to see the sky and sometimes a preponderance of open spaces. Within an hour or so, after traversing a particularly dense section of forest, we came to a larger clearing, illuminated by a shaft of sunlight. We sat in silence for a while beside the stream, now wider, its flow stronger. Khadra found some blackberries nearby and, dividing them into different-sized portions, pretended – amidst laughter and bathed by warm sunshine – to serve us a meal of several courses in a royal palace. Cupping our hands, we drank water from the stream. Khadra played a lively bourrée on her lute. After a while, seeing that the sun was getting lower in the sky, I decided we should press on, in the hope we would find some shelter before nightfall.

As we resumed our journey, a raven swooped low across our path. After performing this manoeuvre several times, it stopped, perching on a low branch some way ahead. It looked intently at us as we approached, its dark eyes menacing in their gaze. As we passed beneath its perch, the bird rose high into the sky. Khadra and the boy quickened their pace. I hurried to keep up and as I did so, stumbled. Once I'd got to my feet, the raven swooped down once more and, to my horror, alighted on my shoulder. I froze in terror as words came from its beak.

"So, Johannes, I see you are still a companion to the girl. And now you have the responsibility of a small boy to care for as well. All such hard, tiring work, is it not? What a burden! It could all have been so much easier, if you had followed my advice. Had you let her go, you could now be enjoying the delights of a beautiful courtesan in La Serenissima – cosseted in the lap of luxury, dressing in fine clothes, no one else to worry about. But, stubborn as always, you turned your back on that prospect for this wretched place. What are we going to do with you?"

"Why do you follow me?" I demanded, trying hard to hide my fear of its proximity – and that of its large black beak – to my face. "I've made my choice on the basis of reason."

"You are not driven by reason, Johannes, but by instinct," replied the raven as it defecated on my shoulder. "The latter is not foolproof. Never was." I tried to dislodge the bird but it clung on defiantly.

"For me, my strongest instinct is my conscience and following my conscience comes from my ability to reason, to know the difference between good and bad. Those who do not reason become slaves, confined to the narrow recesses of a single thought, like you."

The raven sniggered. "Oh Johannes, you are so misguided – the pursuer of rigid principle, unable to weigh everything in the balance, despite your claim to liberating rationality."

In a gesture of profound dislike, I swept the bird from its perch only for it to circle my head and land once more on my shoulder.

"It is you who are misguided," I countered, "pursuing a lost cause. My mind is made up. I know what I have to do."

The raven gave a harsh croak. "Oh Johannes, you fool. We shall see if I'm pursuing a lost cause. There is still far to go before I admit defeat." With those words, the bird leapt into the air and, uttering an eerie laugh, flew up into the trees and disappeared.

"Johannes, who were you talking to?" asked Khadra, waiting for me to catch up.

"No one," I replied, "just the mutterings of a silly old man."

We walked on. Dusk approached and with it crept a chilling mist, its insinuating fingers tugging and dampening our clothes. We began to look for a place to rest and sleep. Before long, we found a small secluded copse of trees with upper branches forming a canopy that might protect us from any rain. We gathered some twigs to make a fire in the hope that I would find the means to create a spark to set them alight. As I struck two stones of flint together, there was movement amongst the adjacent trees. The cart and two horses we had seen earlier emerged from the gloom and drew to a halt. A tall, grey-bearded man got down and walked towards me.

"I've been following you all day," he said. "Not many people pass this way." His face was gaunt, his eyes piercing, his clothing dishevelled.

Khadra and the boy joined us.

"Where are you going?" our visitor asked.

I replied candidly. "We are following the stream, hoping it will lead us to a village or town and perhaps ultimately the sea, where we can find a boat to take us to our destination."

"And what is your destination?"

"The north," Khadra interjected.

The old man looked at us quizzically.

"You have a long way to go. Where have you come from?"

"From the east, across the mountains," Khadra answered.

"How was that possible?" he asked.

"By elephant," she replied.

The old man looked at her intently, appearing for a moment to doubt what she had said, but though his lips moved, there came no response.

We busied ourselves building the pile of twigs to be burned. I resumed my attempt to create a spark from the stones. He spoke again.

"You cannot stay out in the forest. This place is haunted. You had better come with me. My cottage is not far from here. At least you will be safe there. They won't harm you as long as you are with me. I'll lock the door and keep them out."

"Who are 'they'?" Khadra asked.

"I had better not say, lest it frighten your son."

"He is not my son," Khadra quickly replied. "His mother gave him to us for safe keeping."

The man turned his intense look on the boy, but as before said nothing.

We left the copse, with the old man – or Greybeard, as I quietly nicknamed him – leading the horses and cart, now occupied by Khadra and the boy. I tried to find out who "they" were, but he remained silent, seemingly lost in his own thoughts.

His cottage was small, simple in structure, comprising a single room. A fire burned in the centre, a thin spiral of smoke vanishing through an aperture in the roof. Over the flames hung an iron pot into which he put a swiftly prepared mélange of vegetables and rabbit taken from a sack he'd carried from the cart. He barely spoke as he skilfully tended the fire and stirred the pot. We sat close to the flames, warming our cold hands and chilled feet, our hunger keen by the time he gave us each a bowl and an ample helping of the stew. After we had eaten, Khadra played the lute, some gentle melodies which seemed to soothe Greybeard. Later, he untied a bundle of thick sacking and laid out the rough lengths of cloth close to the fire for us to sleep on.

As he did so, an unearthly shriek echoed through the forest. The old man paid no attention, nor did he when another shriek followed. The boy's face turned white in fear. Then came a long, ear-piercing, blood-curdling scream. Khadra's face turned whiter than the boy's.

"What is that?" I asked.

"It's her," replied the old man, almost casually, as he finished laying out the cloth. Again, there came the scream, this time followed by a long, low moan. He looked up at me. "Now you see why it is not wise to sleep under the trees."

"Who? Or should I say, 'What?' for it scarcely sounds human. And why?" I pressed him. He looked into the fire without responding. I asked him again.

"It is the she-wolf, looking for her long-lost cub. Every night she comes and each time she leaves empty-handed, since all she can find are empty graves beneath fallen leaves. Tonight, the moon is high and the higher the moon the greater her anguish, her despair."

"How does her cub come to be missing? Was he taken? Is he dead?"

"No one knows. But she will not give up until she has found him, whether he be dead or alive, and exacted revenge should she learn anyone was responsible."

"What of your horses? Are they safe?"

"Yes, they are safe in their stable. Since they are blind, the she-wolf knows they had no part in what happened."

I urged him several times to tell me what he thought had happened, whether he suspected there was a culprit and who it might be. But he would not say, except to reveal that the she-wolf had frequented the forest for many years and that it might now be her ghost that roamed and howled there every night. He had never actually seen her – or her ghost – so he could not confirm whether the creature we heard was real or a trick of the mind – mere imagination. We slept uneasily that night.

The next morning we rose early, intending, after a rudimentary breakfast, to continue following the stream. But Greybeard would hear none of it. He insisted that we stay longer so he could enjoy our company after so many years of solitude. We helped him to gather mushrooms, and wood for the fire, and picked more blackberries. As evening approached, we sat once again around the fire. He produced more vegetables and another rabbit for the pot, with Khadra contributing some of the mushrooms she had harvested. As his knife skinned, chopped and sliced, he related more tales of the forest and of the city on the far bank of the river of which the stream was a tributary. He promised to accompany us, soon, part of the way in his cart. After we had eaten, Khadra played the lute, including some of the tunes she had played on our way to Jerusalem. The boy sat close to her, staring at the flames hungrily licking the blackened pot.

"Why doesn't the boy speak?" the old man asked. "What is his name?"

I told him what I could. "The boy joined us in Venice. I believe his mother may have been the housekeeper where I lived. She implored us to take him with us. But as for his name, or why he doesn't speak, I'm afraid I don't know."

He beckoned to the child. "Come here."

He was reluctant to leave Khadra's side, but Greybeard persisted, patient, encouraging. "Come and watch me carve." With gentle persuasion from Khadra, the boy got up and with evident lingering apprehension sat next to the old man.

"What shall I make for you?"

The boy looked at him.

"Come, boy, tell me what you would like this piece of wood to become."

The child's lips began to move, to quiver, and then came the words.

"An elephant, please sir."

Khadra and I were astonished to hear him speak.

"What does an elephant look like? I've never seen one. Draw one for me in the ash – here, at the edge of the fire." He handed him a twig, which he had sharpened at one end. The boy took it and, to Khadra's and my further surprise, he drew the faithful outline of an elephant.

"Ah! That's excellent. Thank you. Now I know what it looks like." Greybeard began to carve, the child watching intently as the lump of wood began to take a new shape. Soon, the figure was complete. He gave it to the boy, who immediately rubbed it in the ash.

"Why are you doing that?" the old man asked.

"White. The elephant was white," the boy explained.

Khadra and I listened in amazement.

"Tell me, young man, what is your name?"

"Olfert," followed the answer.

"You must speak more often, Olfert."

The boy did not reply, sitting rapt as Greybeard carved the shape of a wolf.

We fell silent, preferring to watch the old man's deft fingers at work and to listen to the crackle of the fire. Before long, Khadra and Olfert lay down, wrapping themselves in the rough sacking for extra warmth. Within minutes they had fallen asleep. I remained awake, still fascinated by Greybeard's long, gnarled fingers dexterously using the sharp blade to create shape after shape, including that of another – but this time, smaller – wolf. Yet eventually I too began to succumb to fatigue and lay down close to the fire, which was still burning strongly, leaving the old man in a world of his own. Though fatigued, however, I could not sleep, instead turning over and over in my mind where the journey north would take us next and pondering why the boy had suddenly begun to speak.

As I tried to put these thoughts from my head, a shriek similar to those we had heard the night before rent the quietness – but this time it was louder and even more terrifying. I turned. Greybeard was still carving; Khadra and Olfert still slept soundly. Again, the shriek, a piercing cry of agony, followed by the sound of movement outside the cottage. The old man, apparently not aware I was awake, stirred from his fireside reverie, listening intently to the long, low moan of some wretched, heart-wounded being close by. He went and crouched by the door, cupping his hands.

"Hush! He is safe here. You can rest now. Your despair is over."

I heard low sobbing, gradually disappearing, followed by silence. The old man stood and turned towards the fire. I was about to speak but he put his finger to his lips and gestured me to sleep. Neither Khadra nor the boy had stirred.

I woke early, my two companions still asleep, the old man already up.

"Come with me," he whispered.

I followed him outside. Bright, warm sunshine penetrated the forest canopy. We walked some distance.

"She must be here," muttered Greybeard. We walked a little further. He used a shepherd's crook to prod the carpet of golden leaves. "There you are!" he exclaimed. He pointed to a large, grey shape, lifeless at the foot of a great tree. "Here is the she-wolf. She is at peace now. She knows her cub is safe."

I stared at Greybeard, dumbfounded by his words. He took from his pocket the figure of the smaller wolf he had carved the night before and placed it beside the dead animal. He turned to me, saw me struggling to make sense of what he was doing.

"Do you remember the story of the she-wolf that nursed and sheltered Romulus and Remus? She cared for the infants in her lair until they were discovered by the shepherd Faustulus." I nodded but was still unable to articulate the strange notions going through my mind. "I am a descendant of Faustulus," he continued. "Long ago I provided shelter for the boy, Olfert, still asleep in the cottage, after I found them together one day. Then he disappeared. She" – he pointed to the carcass – "and I have been looking for him ever since, wondering where he was and whether he was safe. You and the girl brought him back to the forest so the she-wolf and I could see him for ourselves and be reassured of his well-being. It is his return home, to those who first cared for him, that has enabled him to regain his voice."

I looked at him, speechless, unable to grasp the meaning – if there was one – of what he was saying. Were his words just the deluded ramblings of an old man or did they have a weight and import I should understand? Again he saw my struggle.

"Don't you realise the significance of his name, the name he uttered himself? He said his name was Olfert. It means wolf. The she-wolf lost her cub, but last night, after years of anguished waiting, she discovered he was safe, as I had already done."

After he had covered the dead wolf with leaves, we walked back to the cottage. We did not speak, as however hard I tried I still could not comprehend what the old man had said. Either he was mad or I had lost my sanity.

As we approached the cottage, he placed his arm around my shoulders. "Tomorrow, you will leave for the city – the three of you."

We spent another day helping Greybeard with domestic chores, and that night we sat once more around the fire. The wind picked up and seemed to tug at the roof.

"Have no fear," said the old man. "We are safe."

Rain started to fall, first a light pitter-patter and then harder, drumming a steady, persistent beat on the roof. Khadra, who had been unusually quiet, began to play her lute, the notes soon echoing the insistence of the rain. As the downpour grew heavier, so her music became more strident and intense. Greybeard smiled, Olfert again sitting beside him, watching him carve the figure of a woman, then another and yet another, until there were three standing side by side at the edge of the fire. Khadra played on, her notes still echoing the rhythm of the rain on the roof. I looked at the wooden figures. They began to move in time to her music.

"Look," said Olfert, "they are moving. They are magic!"

"Yes," said the old man, his eyes afire. "They are Furies, dancing in revenge."

I watched incredulous as the female forms stamped their feet to Khadra's music and the percussive beat of the rain.

"What is the cause of their vengeance?" I asked, mesmerised by the movements of the carved women.

"The wrongdoing of a man," he replied casually.

"Which man?" I asked.

"Why you," he replied smiling, his face momentarily mutating into the grinning mask I had seen in Venice.

I froze as he uttered the words.

"You can assuage their fury."

I asked him how.

"You will know soon enough."

Suddenly the rain stopped and Khadra ceased to play. The old man picked up the forms he had so skilfully fashioned.

"Here is one to take as a memento of this night, a reminder on your journey of what you have to do. As for the rest, their job is done." He put the remaining carvings in his pocket.

The next morning we prepared to leave. After an early breakfast, we mounted his cart and set off along a rough track parallel to the stream. An hour or so later, we reached the edge of the forest. Before us the stream had become a wider stretch of muddy water entering a broad river. We could see on the opposite side the distant outline of a castle. The sky was full of small white clouds scudding along in a soft warm breeze.

"There is the boatman waiting for you," said Greybeard, pointing to the nearside bank.

"Thank you for bringing us here," I said, gripping his hand.

"And thank you for your company, for bringing joy to an old man, for Khadra's music and, most of all, for Olfert."

"Thank you, kind sir, for my elephant," added the boy. "It's safely in my pocket."

With a curtsey from Khadra, the three of us took our final leave of the aged man and walked towards the riverbank. As we stepped into the boat, I looked back towards the forest. Greybeard, his horses and cart had disappeared.

"Where do you wish to go, my friends?" asked the boatman.

"Over there, to the city," replied Khadra.

"Let it be so," said the boatman. "There is much to see there."

The boat slipped its mooring and so began the next stage of our journey north.

CHAPTER SEVEN

A Castle of Curiosities

As the boat eased into the current, the far bank appeared close, leading me to think that our passage would be brief. But once out in midstream, instead of heading for the opposite side, the boatman tacked sharply to the right, in a northerly direction, which soon revealed a much wider river than I had thought. Moreover, the wind had strengthened and we were now being borne along at increasing speed. Remembering our earlier voyage across the sea from Palestine, I looked at the nonchalant boatman with some apprehension, wondering what possible fresh tribulations awaited us. He glanced at us, smiled and pointed ahead, mouthing words I found it hard to hear. Seeing I had not heard, he shouted above the rising wind.

"We will soon encounter that part of the river where two stretches of water come together, their currents wrestling with one another for superiority, you might say. But do not worry, you will be safe in my hands."

"How far to where you are taking us?" enquired Khadra, looking nervously at the black seething water, Olfert gripping her hand.

"Perhaps an hour or so's swift sailing," the boatman said, leaning calmly on the tiller.

"Why so long?" I asked.

"This is a mighty river – several miles wide."

"But when we embarked the other side looked so close," I replied, puzzled.

"My friend, many make that mistake. The far bank seemed close because you were looking at an island in the river, not landfall on the far side. You were deceived by an illusion. The island is featureless, flat, barren. No one lives there – it's just a graveyard. We are navigating to the north of it. Once we have rounded its tip, we will encounter the river in its full majesty – vast, unpredictable, petulant, mysterious. Then you will see the far side and the castle, beyond which lies the city. Until we land, hold tight. If you think the present stretch of water is rough, wait until we have left the lee of the island. It will be a contest between us and the forces of nature. I've always won, if that is any comfort to you." He laughed.

High above, the sky was deep blue, small white clouds still drifting lazily from west to east, despite the wind that drove us and in contrast to the river surface, now beginning to bubble furiously like water boiling in a pot. Within a few minutes we approached the tip of the island and the slender boat started to pitch and yaw in the foaming cross-currents. The boatman gripped the tiller, his knees flexing to absorb the uneven movements of his vessel. As we rounded the island's northern headland, a sudden powerful gust of wind struck us amidships, the billowing sail straining to free itself from the slim, bending mast. Khadra, Olfert and I clung tightly both to each other and to the side of the boat, fearing that at any moment we would be hurled into the raging vortex. I looked back at our helmsman. He was laughing as he fought to control the rudder, which struggled to escape his grip. At one point, the boat seemed almost to upend as its hull crashed against a huge black wave before descending, bow down, into the void its force had created. Khadra, Olfert and I grasped even more tightly, Khadra also contending with the wind tugging at the lute slung as usual across her back.

"I won't let you have it. It's mine, not yours," she screamed at the fearsome wind as she pulled the strap closer against her chest.

I turned to look at the island. Immediately beyond the jagged rocks that marked the shoreline, I saw three enormous, hideous gallows, their victims jerking and swinging like marionettes in the gale-force gusts. The gruesome sight made my blood run cold – a reminder of the biblical crucifixion.

Repeatedly, the boat was flung from side to side, but miraculously it withstood the river's anger. Once more the boatman sought to reassure us.

"Have no fear! We'll reach our destination. The currents and the wind are unusually strong today, but my sturdy boat will not be deflected. Hold –" But the boatman's hollered words were again lost in another tortured howl of ferocious wind.

The journey continued in this manner for what seemed an eternity. But once we were in the lee of the approaching land, a gentle breeze replaced the brutal buffeting and the turbulent surface of the water became a pane of glistening glass. Drenched, we sat without speaking in warm sunlight, thankful that we had survived, still clutching the gunwale of the boat as it edged into a small steep-sided harbour. Its uneven contours were lined with small houses painted in all colours of the rainbow.

Once the boat was secured, we took our leave of the boatman. He said nothing as he helped Khadra and Olfert set foot on the narrow stone jetty. As I disembarked, I lost my footing but was saved from falling into the water by the boatman's vice-like grip on my arm. Recovering my balance, I turned to thank him, only to see for a few fleeting moments the smiling mask I had twice encountered in Venice. It whispered in my ear.

"Another close shave, Johannes. Why do you expose yourself to such risks for the sake of that girl and the boy? You think you and she are bound by an unbreakable bond of deep friendship. You are mistaken. Mark my words, it will snap easily enough. She'll leave you for some handsome young man, as she nearly did in La Serenissima. Then what will you do – all alone, unable to get back to where you first saw her?"

The dark, chilling eyes looked intently into mine but I said nothing. As the boatman let go of my arm, the masked face disappeared. The boatman pointed to a narrow, winding pathway leading from the jetty up a steep hill, on top of which stood a great stone pillar. Once again troubled by what I had just seen, I thanked him for his good seamanship and offered him money for his pains. But he pushed my hand away. As I quickly followed Khadra and the boy, he called out.

"Go to the castle. There you will find shelter before your onward journey. Good luck." He waved, throwing his head back in guffaws of laughter.

Khadra, Olfert and I walked slowly up the precarious, increasingly steep pathway, past houses barely large enough for one person to live in, let alone two. Wisps of smoke coiled lazily towards the sky from their chimneys. But we saw no one. Eventually, reaching the summit of the hill, we stood on the base of the pillar – on top of which was a stone pelican, feeding its chicks with its own blood – and looked down to the harbour. I saw that the river we had crossed was indeed many miles wide, saw the grim island in the middle and, in the far distance, the river bank from which we had set out. The boat that had brought us was edging out of the harbour, back in the direction from which we had come.

As the sun was beginning to set, and feeling chilled in our damp clothes, we had little choice but to press on. The pathway widened into a road deeply rutted by cart tracks. In the distance, perhaps two or so miles away, was the castle. We walked quickly towards it, passing through seemingly deserted villages. Nearing the stronghold, I saw that its huge walls emerged from vast granite rocks, which formed one side of a broad moat. We followed a track along the moat edge until we came to a lowered drawbridge. Crossing it, we arrived at an immense wooden gate, a long thick rope hanging to one side. I pulled it. A deep sonorous toll rang out from a large bell above, echoing within the castle and without. As the last echo of the bell faded, I heard bolts being unfastened and the gate slowly opened, revealing an inner archway and, beyond it, the walls of a great central bastion, the entrance to which was approached by a wide stone slope. Passing under the archway, I saw that adjacent to the slope was a chapel with huge Gothic windows. Now closer, I stood amazed by the size and height of the central tower. We walked towards it, my companions clearly sharing my nervousness, and, as we did so, another large door at the top of the slope, beneath the image of a double-headed eagle, swung open. As one, we hesitated to go further.

"Well, aren't you going to enter?" a voice boomed from an embrasure above us. "Hurry, the door won't stay open while you gawp."

Still, we hesitated.

Again, the voice boomed. "If you don't enter quickly, the door will close. Then what will you do?"

I summoned my courage and entered, Khadra and Olfert following close behind. After passing through a long tunnel flanked by guards dressed in black-and-red doublets, we emerged into an inner courtyard. It was a scene of much hustle and bustle – pigs and chickens running loose, a blacksmith at work and women washing clothes. To one side were several carts loaded with a bewildering variety of objects of all shapes, sizes and purposes. We stood in the midst of this frenetic activity, unsure where to go or what to do next. Suddenly, a small white-haired man, dressed in green and black, emerged from the hubbub. As he approached us, he did three somersaults, to Olfert's astonished delight.

"Sorry about that but I have to stay fit if I am to keep up with my master's demands. Follow me. The Emperor is expecting you. My name is Osbaldo, by the way."

We followed our guide, who continued to turn somersaults, along interminable corridors and through high-vaulted galleries, each full of cupboards with doors securely padlocked and labelled in an indecipherable script. We passed through a great hall, a huge fire burning in the vast hearth, into a smaller antechamber. At the far end sat an elderly man in a majestic, throne-like chair. He was dressed in a long, capacious blue robe; his red-cheeked face was framed by flowing white hair that reached his shoulders. On a table in front of him were stacks of enormous ledgers. He rose to greet us.

"Welcome to my castle – to my cabinet of curiosities, as I prefer to call it. I believe I have the pleasure of meeting Mister Johannes, Mistress Khadra and young Master Olfert. Am I rightly informed?"

"Yes, sir," replied Olfert.

"I'm pleased to hear that, young man. Let us eat, then we will sit by the fire and you can tell me your story. But first, my servants will find you fresh clothes."

*

After supper, we sat around the fire in the great hall and told him of our travels. When we had finished, and without any comment on his part, he asked Khadra to play, not her lute, but a beautiful guitar which he took down from its niche above the fireplace.

"Please play me something soothing, melodic. Do you sing?"

Khadra nodded.

"I'm an old man – very ancient, as you can see – a collector of things, memories, the idiosyncrasies of others. Your music, your voice, Mistress Khadra, will become, I'm sure, one of my treasured recollections. Because I have gathered so many things and read so many books, I will have much to draw on during my eventual journey through eternity."

Playing the instrument with ease, Khadra sang from her treasured Dowland book.

> *Come again!*
> *Sweet love doth now invite*
> *Thy graces that refrain*
> *To do me due delight,*
> *To see, to hear, to touch, to kiss, to die,*
> *With thee again in sweetest sympathy.*

As she sang further verses, I gazed at her. The clothes she had been given were of a style from an earlier age but they suited her slim figure exquisitely. She wore a full-length off-white décolleté silk gown beneath a loose, sleeveless, powder-blue cutaway overgown drawn together by wide blue ribbon beneath her bust. Her hair was pinned up. Olfert stood by her side, turning the pages.

"Mistress Khadra, that was splendid. Now, please play me some tunes on your lute."

For the next hour or so, she played, often improvising. The lute echoed throughout the great hall, the old man gazing into the flames as though recalling memories, some sweet, some sad, judging by the occasional shedding of a tear.

*

The following morning, while the Emperor still slept, Osbaldo took us on a tour of the castle. From the ramparts, we could see on one side the river we had crossed and on the other, a city, stretching far into the distance.

"His Imperial Majesty's realm lies before you," said Osbaldo, "but on account of his age and the tireless pursuit of his collectibles, as he calls them, he sees little of his subjects. They are pleased that is the case. His taxes are high but other than that they are happy to be left to their own devices."

"What does he collect – apart, of course, from taxes?" Khadra asked.

"Everything. Nothing is excepted. Even the dress you wore last night – he collected that from the resplendent court at Versailles, where it was alleged to have been made for one of the King's beauties. But she fell out of favour and it was never worn."

Khadra persisted with her questions. "If the Emperor rarely travels, how does he find things to collect?"

"He sits at his desk daily and sends out instructions to his many agents and messengers, describing in great detail what he wishes them to find. As he is an emperor, who can refuse him?" replied Osbaldo.

"May we see some of what he has collected?" Khadra asked.

"But of course!" Osbaldo answered.

And so began our remarkable journey through the castle's interior. Instead of flamboyantly displayed emblems of imperial power, there were endless, bare-walled, characterless corridors and rooms containing nothing but cabinets. Osbaldo pulled behind him a small handcart laden with keys to open each one. We saw natural minerals such as hardstones, coral and rock crystal; rhinoceros horns; sculptures in stone and silver, one of the latter depicting Daphne with her hair being transformed into the laurel of ancient mythology, while one of the former was of a woman wearing a bodice covered in mussel shells and an underskirt decorated with polished oyster shells. A roomful of cabinets contained a multiplicity of other shells, some minute, some large, including one that, according to Osbaldo, transported Venus. Other cupboards revealed stuffed birds and animals, including a bear and a crocodile, both of which terrified Olfert. In yet further cabinets were the spoils of hunting, especially mutilated and deformed antlers. A sequence of corridors held large cabinets containing arrays of gowns, made from silk and other exotic fabrics, and hats, hairpieces and shoes. Similar cupboards were crammed with elaborate clothes for men. Passageway after passageway, room after room, the collection went on, covering the gamut of music, art and science. Eventually, we came to an iron grille through which we could see a flight of stairs.

"Where do those steps lead to?" I asked.

"They descend to my master's museum of the mind," said Osbaldo. "But there is no time to show you that now. He will have woken and will have fresh instructions to issue. Mistress Khadra, he wishes you to play for him again this evening, as do we all. Come and sit in the castle garden. With such unseasonably warm weather, you can rest in comfort there. The gardener, a woman of great knowledge and passion for her chosen métier, will provide you with refreshment and show you some of the plants and insects the master has collected."

In a matter of seconds, which completed the bafflement of my sense of orientation, Osbaldo led us out of the castle. Opening a heavy oak door adjacent to one of the towers in the domineering defences, he showed us into a secluded walled garden in which were planted an array of colourful flowers, some familiar to me, others more unusual and exotic. The parterre was surrounded by a narrow border of rich green lawn. In one corner of the garden were a small fountain and a moss-covered basin, in the shape of a lion's face, set into the wall. In another corner was an old lime tree, planted, Osbaldo said, by an empress long ago. Close to the tree, a woman was tending a shrub.

"Ah! There she is. That's Agneta, the Emperor's gardener," declared Osbaldo, clapping his hands in an exuberant gesture of delight.

The woman straightened and turned. Tall and imposing, she walked towards us.

With a joyful flourish, Osbaldo effected the introductions.

"Agneta, this is Herr Johannes and Mistress Khadra. They are guests of the Emperor. Mistress Khadra is an accomplished player of the lute and much pleases His Majesty."

"Welcome to my personal fiefdom. It is an honour to greet you."

"It is our pleasure to be here," replied Khadra. "Please, tell us more about your realm."

"In accordance with the Emperor's wishes, I have laid out the garden by theme and colour. It is perhaps too small for the ever-growing size of the collection – varieties of fragrant plants and herbs that are tolerant of drought because not far beneath the soil is granite rock. Many specimens have come from distant places, brought to me by imperial messengers, as directed by His Majesty. I can show you more, if you so wish."

"Yes, please," said Khadra excitedly.

As we wandered around the garden, Agneta described in exact and loving detail the contents of each of the parterre's beds.

"And over here," she said, concluding our tour, "I have created a concealed inset in the wall to serve as a place for insects such as bees and beetles to inhabit if they do not wish to frequent the plants. As for the lime tree, the Emperor likes to sit beneath it to commemorate the summer solstice."

"How long have you been mistress of this enviable sanctuary?" I asked.

"I have been in the Emperor's employment for several years. I hope he will soon release me to travel to faraway countries so I can personally select additions to this collection that I think would please him greatly. I invite you to sit by the tree and enjoy the garden while I fetch you some refreshment. It is such a pleasure to have visitors. There have been so few in the past."

While she and Osbaldo entered a cottage on the far side of the garden, approached through a low doorway, Khadra and I sat alone, listening to the hum of the bees, a songful blackbird in the lime tree and the sound of the fountain's trickling water.

"This reminds me of the perfumed garden in Jerusalem."

"Yes," replied Khadra. "And the scent of the flowers brings back memories of my childhood in the East."

I turned to reply but she placed a pre-emptive hand on mine.

"Hush, Johannes. Let's enjoy the peace and solitude."

Before long Agneta reappeared, with Osbaldo at her side bearing a tray on which were small silver cups.

"These contain juices made from the fruits of the garden. Please enjoy one."

She sat beside us, Osbaldo taking his leave to return to the Emperor.

"Madame, your garden is a true paradise," said Khadra with a sigh of contentment. "Did you know that our term for a place of heavenly bliss such as this evolved from an Old Persian word meaning a walled garden? And your love of the garden is evident."

"Thank you," replied Agneta. "It is indeed the object of my undivided devotion."

"Tell us more of your story," I requested.

"My father died when I was very young. My stepfather, a painter of flowers and still lifes, encouraged me to draw and paint. I also became fascinated by insects, in particular how caterpillars became butterflies and moths. Silk worms also became a passion. Later, I married. My husband always urged me to continue capturing nature on paper and canvas. After he died, just a year after our wedding, I began to teach young girls from wealthy families to be equally interested in the portrayal of the natural world. I became well known, leading to the Emperor's invitation, which I gladly accepted."

"Do you have paintings I could see?" asked Khadra.

"Of course. I will be honoured to show you. They are in the cottage, if you would like to accompany me there."

I sat alone in the garden, lost in thought in the late-afternoon sun. Sometime later, Khadra and Agneta reappeared, arm in arm, chatting and laughing as though they had long been the closest of friends. As we left the garden, Khadra remarked, "I hope that my mother, if I ever find her, will be as kind and warm-hearted as Agneta."

Early that evening, we joined the Emperor for a banquet, attended by nobles, imperial envoys and ambassadors from far-off territories.

The plate on the table was gold, the food extravagant and the wine rich in taste. Once the table had been cleared, the hall was set for a tableau, a depiction of the Adoration of the Magi, to mark the approaching Advent. The Emperor clapped his hands to gain attention.

"I have a new collectible. She is the beautiful Mistress Khadra – from Palestine, no less – who will provide musical accompaniment on her lute. Please, Mistress Khadra, begin."

Khadra took her place and began to play as the Holy Family assembled and the enactment began. For the arrival of the magi, she chose music I had heard her play on the shore of the Sea of Galilee. The audience sat enraptured, as much by the music and the musician as by the unfolding tableau. I knew the Emperor's request would be causing her considerable discomfort because the scene would be a bitter reminder of the image of the Virgin in the locket around her neck, which she had thought was of her mother. But whatever the degree of her sorrow she disguised it.

The evening's entertainment lasted many hours and it was not until after midnight that the Emperor withdrew, thus permitting his many guests to depart. We sat alone by the fire, the boy soon falling asleep, Khadra and I deciding how best to break the news to the Emperor that we wished to continue our journey to the north the next day.

Osbaldo came to place more wood on the fire.

"Now your master has gone to bed, may we see his museum of the mind?" asked Khadra.

"Are you sure that is what you wish to do?"

Dismissing the caution in Osbaldo's question she replied crisply, "Yes, it is."

I placed my hand on Khadra's arm, meaning to divert her resolve by pointing out how late it was, but she gently removed it. "I wish to go, even if Herr Johannes does not. We'll leave Olfert asleep by the fire."

"Since you are determined, I will accompany you," I assured her.

"Then let us go – without delay," said Osbaldo.

Taking a flaming torch from the wall, he led us back to the great metal grille. He unlocked it, and we followed him slowly down the twisting steps. At the bottom of the staircase, Osbaldo tied one end of a reel of thick wool to an iron ring in the wall. Then he took two more torches from their sconces, lit them from his, and handed one to each of us. "Stay close to me," he instructed. We walked along a long, bleak, cold corridor. As he passed another iron ring in the wall, he threaded the reel of wool through it and so with the next ring and the one after that.

"Why are you doing that?" I asked uneasily.

"So we can find our way back!" he replied sharply.

I was about to ask how many had been lost because they'd been unable to find their way back, but he forestalled me.

"Please, do not talk further. I must concentrate. I have no wish to see us trapped."

Khadra pulled me close to her and felt for my hand, holding it tightly. It was the first time I had felt her so near to me. Her shiver ran equally through me.

"Do you wish to continue?" Osbaldo asked, sensing our increasing discomfort.

"Yes," replied Khadra in a bold voice.

We walked on, Osbaldo still periodically threading the wool through iron rings, until eventually we came to another flight of steps. He descended, with us close behind him.

"Wait here!" he ordered.

A minute or so later, torches on the wall burst into flame revealing a cavernous chamber. In it was a low stone maze, its passages, lined with indistinct yet grotesque images, twisting and turning in different directions, apparent staircases descending into the darkness below. In the silence, I heard distant sounds of anguish.

"This is the Emperor's museum of the mind," said Osbaldo. "My master has in his most secret cabinet, near to where he sleeps, a human skull and, beside it, a brain, removed after death and preserved. Fascinated by these objects and the powers and functions they represent, he wanted to replicate the brain here, beneath the castle, so he could study how it works and, indeed, experiment. He believes the human brain is a maze, that though our minds are unlimited in scope and imagination, our freedom to achieve what we seek is denied by our fears, limitations, contradictions and cowardice. He wanted to study how people behave in certain situations. In this maze, you can go forward yet be tricked into going sideways, use the staircases in search of liberation yet each one proving to be an illusion. In the Emperor's opinion, if we want to retreat – to begin again or to go in a different direction – it is hard to do so unless there is a thread to enable us to escape to a new freedom, to a liberated mind."

I was lost for words. The maze in front of us, illuminated by the flickering torchlight, was shadow-filled and menacing. Khadra gripped my hand even tighter.

"The experiments," I began, "what were they? Have they been successful? Has all this" – my gesture took in the whole dismal chamber – "achieved its purpose, been worth it?"

"He built the maze at great cost and with the loss of several lives in order to see his victims try to escape and, when they couldn't, thus prove to them that they were dependent on him. He's like the Minotaur – he devours people. Beyond the wall at the far end is yet another staircase, leading to cells where it is said those who have gone mad seeking to escape his grip are kept. But I consider that unlikely – the Minotaur devoured people, it did not keep them alive. In the cabinets above, all is lifeless. Here in this maze – this replica, according to my master, of the human mind – he puts the living to the test to prove the fragility of that mind and, of course, to demonstrate his victims' dependence on him, sometimes to the point of devouring them. I pity him because in his old age he does not know, cannot accept, that he has been driven to madness by his own experiment. He has become all-consumed by his passion to collect and study. What he wants, he gets. What he likes, he keeps. But he is as trapped as any of his collectibles. He has been devoured by his own Minotaur – his collection."

"Osbaldo, let us return to the castle above," I urged. "We have seen enough of this hideous place."

"Of course, but I have a word of warning for you, Mistress

Khadra. The Emperor has fallen under the spell of your music and he has already identified you as a prized living collectible for his musical museum. That surely means he will be most reluctant to let you leave. He will certainly condemn you to play for him every day, and perhaps exercise other seigneurial rights by night as well. This evening, he will ask you to play again, just to him, so that he can make a final judgement as to your value before he enters your name into his ledger. Mistress, play your most bewitching music and then, when he has fallen asleep, you, Mister Johannes and the boy must flee the castle. I will prepare a carriage to take you."

During the ensuing day, we busied ourselves as best we could in the castle garden and in the gardener's house, I, for one, never quite managing to eradicate my awareness of the risk we were about to take. Late in the afternoon, Osbaldo came to tell Khadra that the Emperor had chosen a new gown for her to wear. She should go and put it on, ready for the Emperor's approval.

Shortly after seven o'clock, when the castle had fallen quiet, the Emperor summoned us to his presence and, after a brief supper, we sat once more before the great hearth. He and Khadra sat opposite each other; Olfert and I looked on from a slight distance. The gown he had selected for her, worn over a low-cut undergown of deep red, was of white silk with intricate patterns outlined in gold embroidery. It had a high collar and its long train was cast across the stone floor like an incoming tide, edging towards her chair and footstool. Her hair was again pinned tightly up, held in place by golden combs. She was dressed like a bride before committal.

The Emperor observed her closely, gazing at her long fingers as they nimbly plucked the lute strings. As during the tableau, Khadra interspersed her repertoire with some of the melodies I had heard her play in Palestine. I watched her in awe. I could scarcely believe that, not long before, when I first encountered her in the cathedral, this woman had been a mere child. The more I took in her beauty, and recalled her hand holding mine the night before, the more I realised I was possibly falling in love with her bewitching allure, so breaking the vow I had made in Venice. The Emperor leaned forward, mesmerised by her, touching her hand as she ceased one piece of music and turned the page of her Dowland book to play another. She did not respond to his gesture as she had done to the handsome young nobleman in the Doge's Palace.

She played long into the night and again it was past midnight before the Emperor stirred from his chair and retired, followed by Osbaldo. Khadra continued to play until Osbaldo returned.

"Come with me, quickly. The Emperor is asleep but he has asked me to wake him early so that he can formally appoint you his court musician, Mistress Khadra."

We followed him down several flights of stairs until we came to a large wooden door. He drew back the heavy, freshly greased bolts.

"Outside is a carriage bearing the imperial coat of arms. It will take you to a city in a valley beyond the boundaries of the Emperor's power, where I hope both of you will find peace of mind."

I spoke for all of us. "Thank you, Osbaldo, for your great kindness and advice. We will long remember your generosity."

He opened the door and, after quickly shedding her white overgown and donning a deep-green hooded cloak proffered by Osbaldo, Khadra, Olfert and I stepped into the waiting black carriage.

Waving him goodbye, we crossed the drawbridge and then gathered speed as we began our journey across the dark landscape towards the distant valley. As we left behind the last houses of the Emperor's city, I noticed a flickering reflection through the small window at the back of the carriage. We turned. The castle tower was alight, flames gouging their way through the windows. I thought I could hear great shrieks of imperial rage as fire consumed a lifetime of strange collectibles. I could not bear to think of the occupants of the cells beyond the maze. Or were they the imagination of an unsound mind? Agneta, her paintings and garden were indisputably real, however, and I could see that the thought she and they might perish in the conflagration added to Khadra's horror even more than it did my own. But we could not go back.

CHAPTER EIGHT

The Commission

I cannot say how long we slept, except to record that nothing on our sudden flight through the night in the imperial coach caused us to wake. I was the first to stir. I lifted the window blind. Drifts of late-autumn leaves from the trees lining the road covered the ground. The landscape was undulating but largely featureless. Distant hills were barely visible on the horizon. Khadra was still deeply asleep beside me, wrapped in my cloak as well as her own. Olfert lay in a similar state of slumber on the opposite bench, visibly taller than I remembered from a day or so before. Whether we were travelling in a northerly or easterly direction remained a matter of conjecture until the layer of light but effectively sun-obscuring cloud cleared.

As we sped on, I tried to concentrate on my overwhelming desire to return to the place I had left so long ago. I had lost all sense of time and orientation, repeatedly confused by what was happening and where I was going. I longed for the certainty I had once possessed. I seemed to be walking on shifting sands, uncertain of my footing. Moreover, I had this heavy responsibility – to help Khadra find her mother. As for Olfert, he had no mother to search for. Instead, he required the comfort and security of a home where, in due course, he could decide what he wished to make of his life. The carriage gently swayed as I tried hard to make sense of and impose order on my predicament.

"Well, Johannes, here you are again – still journeying to the north, still bearing self-imposed responsibility for the woman beside you and for a callow youth as well. What a heavy burden you carry, and for what purpose?"

I could not find where the voice was coming from. I lifted the blind to see if we were being followed by the bird that had dogged my heels in the forest. We were not. And neither Khadra nor Olfert bore a smiling mask.

"What an escape you had last night! Who is the all-consuming Minotaur in your life? Her? The boy? Or is the Minotaur your own stubbornness, your refusal to bend?"

Once more, I looked out of the window to see where the voice – so clear and close – was coming from.

"Johannes, stop looking for me. I'm in your head. I am your thoughts." The voice laughed.

"Leave me in peace!" I cried.

"One minute I am in your head. Now, I am your coachman. Next, your boatman, a raven, a mask. I am everywhere."

I covered my ears to rid myself of the voice but to no avail.

"Johannes, your silence speaks volumes. Remember the maze in the castle. Imagine it in your mind – those twisting, turning paths, those staircases to nowhere. You are groping in the darkness towards the centre, unable to avoid an inevitable, logical outcome. Within the hour you will be at your next destination. There you will have another opportunity to decide what to do. Think carefully, Johannes, think very carefully about what you desire – a tortured mind or freedom."

"Leave me be! I will decide my fate, not you."

"Who was that talking?" asked Khadra as she stirred.

"The coachman. He said we are nearing our destination."

"It sounded like your voice."

"You were mistaken. It was the coachman. I merely thanked him."

As the voice had predicted, soon the carriage crossed a wide, imposing stone bridge and a few minutes later stopped in a main city square. Disembarking, I saw a pleasing scene – residential quarters to the right and to the left the river and beyond it a wide valley with what I took to be vineyards on the far hillside; beyond those were steeper hills. On the northern side of the square was the old town – the Altstadt – with a skyline of church spires, domes and towers. Within the square itself, travellers were coming and going, by coach, by horse and on foot. Amongst them were merchants, craftsmen and apprentices, farmers and beggars, each engaged in their respective transactions. I turned to say farewell to the coachman but he had already disappeared in the mêlée.

As we were pondering in which direction we should go, a well-presented man in court dress emerged from the throng of people.

"Let me introduce myself. I am Griebel." Doffing his hat, he bowed. "Welcome to our city. You must be Herr Johannes?" I nodded. "And do I have the pleasure of greeting Mistress Cecilia?" asked Griebel, referring to the baptismal name Khadra had been given at the *seminario* in Venice.

Khadra curtsied demurely in reply, then added, "And this is Olfert."

"Your son, madame?" Griebel asked quickly.

"No, he is not my son but, like Herr Johannes, a pleasurable companion."

"Thank you for the clarification. I've come not only to greet you but to convey an invitation from my master, His Excellency the Duke, to play for him. He is a much-admired patron of the musical arts and has heard many accounts of your prowess as a lutenist. In two days' time there will be a festival to mark the commencement of Advent, including a concert in the Hofkirche performed by an orchestra of great talent. It would please His Excellency if you were to join them with your lute."

"I would be greatly honoured," answered Khadra without hesitation.

"Good," said Griebel. "Then everything is agreed. Please follow me and I will show you to the lodgings we have arranged for you in Taschenbergstrasse, where you will find all the comforts you require after a long journey."

The rooms were indeed well-appointed and spacious, evidently part of an old palace. We quickly settled in.

Later in the day, Olfert and I walked along a broad terrace

overlooking the placid river that meandered its way through the city, frequently fascinated by the myriad small vessels traversing it. As we strolled, I was struck by the large, impressive buildings rising high above us on our right, amongst which, we learned from a passer-by, were the Duke's palace, a grand library and, the most daunting-looking, a guard house. Beyond was a bridge. Further along the terrace there were enormous stone figures representing the parts of the day and the months of the year. Each one we passed was, for me, a reminder of the passage of time. Olfert's concern, meanwhile, was the future.

"Where will we go next?" he asked.

"When the time is right, we will travel further north – to my homeland."

"How much further is that?"

"I do not know. I have no map but I believe we have made progress."

The boy had evidently been storing up his questions.

"What will happen when we reach the north?"

"I will be able to reflect on a long and strange journey and, of course, on the pleasure of your and Khadra's companionship."

"And what will happen to me and Khadra when you reach your destination?"

"I cannot say for certain, Olfert. But I hope that you will find a trade as an apprentice and, once you have completed your apprenticeship, that you will be able to settle down and one day achieve great fame and fortune."

"And Khadra, what of her?" he asked.

"She is searching for someone, and hopes she will find that someone in the north."

"Who might that be?" Olfert looked briefly dejected, as though disappointed that his companionship might not be enough.

"Her mother," I replied.

"Will she find her?"

"Again, I do not know. But if she does not, she has already found something of value – that is, skill and fame as a musician. Where that path might lead next is also unknown, at least for the present."

"And –"

I put my hand on his shoulder.

"See, we have already reached the statue of evening, judging by the candle she holds. It is time we returned to our lodgings to spend time with Khadra."

But when we arrived, she was not there, instead returning much later.

The next day, while Khadra, at the Duke's instigation, was fitted for a new gown, Olfert and I went to the church where she would perform with the Duke's chamber orchestra. As we turned the corner of the street, I could see the Hofkirche was a splendid symbol of the Catholic creed; the high, finely structured spire a physical manifestation of its power. Inside, the nave was long, with two side aisles and two corner chapels. Beyond the nave was an elaborate stone-carved rood screen and beyond that the choir and the high altar. As we walked slowly towards the transept, I noticed sandstone bas-reliefs decorating the balustrades of an overhead gallery on either side. Above the high altar was a breathtaking painting of the crucifixion and Christ's ascent into heaven. Around the massive depiction were an array of complex and finely worked side panels, telling the story of His life. I stood transfixed by the images and their rich colours.

"I wonder how long it took to paint," said Olfert.

"That would depend on many factors," I began. "For example –"

"Impressive, is it not?" said a voice behind me. I turned to see a man in later years – tall, distinguished and, from the cut and quality of his clothes, a man of some wealth. His dusty boots suggested he had been travelling and was therefore perhaps a visitor rather than a resident of the city.

"Indeed it is," I replied. "It is the kind of work of art I would like to paint myself."

"Why do you say that?"

"I have painted – mostly portraits for those who wish to display their place in society. But the piece before us enabled the painter to leave his mark for generations to come. It was clearly a challenge and he, the artist, met it, in my estimation, with resounding success. For myself, I seek a similar challenge – the opportunity to demonstrate my skills and leave a visible legacy. However, I fear the time for such an opportunity has long since passed. Now, we will leave you to admire the painting in peace. I wish you good day, sir."

But the man walked with us. "Are you a painter of note?"

"No, I cannot claim that to be the case. Nowadays, I paint fewer portraits – occasionally street scenes. It does not earn much, but sufficient to provide food at home. Though," I added, "I have not painted for some while."

"Then you would not be interested in our search for an artist of some accomplishment to paint a large picture for us."

"I should like to know more, before deciding whether that is so," I replied.

"I am Jacob Hendricks, a merchant with many interests in a city to the north of this one. I travel here frequently, to buy and sell, and always come to the Hofkirche before I leave to admire this altarpiece." We turned to look back at it. "Soon my guild will have sufficient money to commission a large painting for our guildhall."

"Do you have a subject in mind?"

"We are men of commerce. We pay our dues to the city and give alms to the poor. With that in mind, we desire a painting that will depict Christ's utterance, 'Render unto Caesar the things that are Caesar's and unto God the things that are God's.' An image, grand in scale, that will show us law-abiding to the civil power but mindful of our religious duty to help those less fortunate than us with good works. We intend to pay well."

"Have you had many seekers of this commission?"

"Some, but it behoves us, the council, to consider others before making our decision. If you are interested in such a commission, then we would ask that you submit samples of your work." He pulled a small dog-eared leaflet from his pocket and thrust it into my hand. "There, something to think about. Good day to you." Raising his hat, he quickly turned on his heel and walked away before I could tell him my name.

Olfert and I lingered for a few more moments to gaze at the

altarpiece – to marvel at its scale, intricacy and majesty.

"I have seen you sketch people and street scenes on scraps of paper, heard the compliments you receive. Perhaps you should seek the commission?" said Olfert.

"I may be an artist who can capture everyday life, but I am not an artist who can paint a large canvas fit to hang in a public place. Besides, why should I paint a picture to show the humbug of merchants who think that hanging such a work in their guildhall will help assuage their selfish love of wealth?"

"Perhaps you and I should work together and submit?"

I laughed. "Olfert, we do not have the skills required."

"Let us try, sir. Please."

I did not reply.

Early the following afternoon, people began to gather for the evening's courtly festivities to mark the start of Advent. Mingling with the well-dressed and important were minstrels, musicians, dancers and clowns. In the streets close to the Hofkirche, there were stalls displaying the wares of an array of craftsmen and tradespeople, including goldsmiths and silversmiths. Even closer to the church, an exotic wooden pavilion had been constructed. Inside was a giant wooden sculpture of nymphs bathing amidst jets of water, which those attending the concert filed past as they processed into the church to take their seats before the Duke's arrival. Inside the Hofkirche itself, rows of benches had been placed the length of the nave. By the rood screen a large, ornately carved wooden throne had been set, ready for the Duke. Olfert and I found our seats in the side aisle and a short while afterwards, the small orchestra took up position.

Almost an hour later, the ducal procession arrived, descending a staircase from an upper passage connected to the Duke's residence. Taking his place, the Duke signalled the concert should begin.

I listened intently as the orchestra played three concertos, the harmonies of each movement, whether it be allegro, adagio or vivace, echoing through the high-vaulted nave. The musicians were encircled by candles, their light casting flickering shadows on the pillars. Surrounded by violinists and cellists, Khadra, striking in a black gown edged with gold, the richly varied shades of her pinned-back hair catching in the candlelight, played her lute with flawless exactitude, her fingers caressing the strings. After the concert, Khadra's performance was acclaimed. As in Venice, she became the talk of the city. The completion of our journey north would have to wait.

In the days that followed, I still struggled to orientate myself and acclimatise – I saw some similarities with all I had known in my old life, but fewer in number compared to dissimilarities – and sometimes to hold on to my identity. Often, in my sleep, I thought I was still on the boat from Palestine, alone and drifting aimlessly on a windless sea with no sight of land, lost in limbo. By day, I tried to stay occupied, but when neither Khadra nor Olfert were present, I frequently looked at the leaflet Jacob Hendricks had given me, increasingly tempted to seek their prize.

Olfert and I made the acquaintance of a painter, Master Gysbert, commissioned by the Duke to produce a portrait of Khadra. He quickly executed the work on an oval canvas, presenting his subject half-turned to the viewer, holding her lute. His brushstrokes were loose but showed exquisite command of tone, particularly in the portrayal of her dress and skin colour. It was a style I now sought to emulate; should I master it, I would apply the technique in the picture I executed were I to win the commission. When the artist was not present, Olfert and I used his studio, I to paint from my quick pencil sketches of the city and its inhabitants, and he to create river scenes from his own drawings. Olfert's newly acquired skill was remarkable, not least the delicacy of the colours he mixed for my palette. Before long I had completed, with his assistance, a series of small paintings which won the praise of Gysbert. The next day I reread the now crumpled piece of paper given me by Hendricks and decided I would seek the commission.

However, mindful of my promise to Khadra to help her find her mother, and unsure of where I was in the span of time – how long our journey had taken so far and would still take, how long the commission would require – I could not easily see when we might leave for Hendricks' city in order to present my pictures to his guild. Should I travel alone, or with Olfert? Leave Khadra behind, or persuade her to travel with us? My return journey north was incomplete, the route still shrouded in mystery, and I had promised Khadra my companionship and assistance in her search for her mother, a task that still preoccupied her mind. We both therefore still needed the support we each looked for from the other. But, equally, I was becoming increasingly obsessed with the commission. Was I selfish in this obsession, obstructing Khadra's quest? Or was I on the brink of acknowledging that the man in the smiling mask was right, that my companionship with her should end? Several times I was on the brink of asking her whether we should part, but each time I lacked the courage to speak.

One night, in the darkest small hours, I woke to find two figures at the foot of my bed. The first was Khalid, the other a woman, wrapped in a cloak and with silver hair beneath a fine veil.

"Mister Johannes," said Khalid, "we have heard of the great praise for our daughter, Khadra, for her beauty and her music. We miss her, and the magic of her oud. We urge you to persuade her to return to play for us and thus bring us great comfort. Her music was incomparable."

"Khalid," I replied, "Khadra is no longer the child you knew. She is now a woman and I cannot persuade her to do what she does not want to do. She left you to find her mother. While she has discovered the joy and power of music and enjoys a growing reputation, she has still not found her. I promised to help. The search must continue. It is my obligation to see that it does."

"But which is more important, her fame or her people?" he pleaded.

"I cannot answer such a question. Only she can. I would only say, though it pains me to do so, she is not one of your people. Those she is amongst here, they are her own people."

Khalid's face slowly disappeared into the darkness.

The veiled woman spoke.

"Herr Johannes, Mistress Khadra has great skill as a musician.

She needs to share her gift more widely and to increase its scope and value by composing her own music, not merely performing that of others. She should continue her journey north, where I know someone of great influence who can help her take her accomplishments to greater heights – not in provincial towns but in great cities and royal courts. Then perhaps one day, when she is truly famous, she can return to where she took you on that voyage through the night."

With those words the woman vanished too. Barely had she gone when the curtain around my bed rustled, pulled back by the man in the smiling mask.

"So, Johannes, what are you going to do? Persuade her to return to Palestine, or to go north? Surely the time has come for you to let her go and to summon the courage to continue your journey, and pursue the commission, unencumbered, without her. You cannot keep her, cling to her. Poor Johannes. What a decision you have to make. There is no escape. You must decide."

"You hideous, unwelcome creature! Why do you plague me? I will complete my journey and Khadra will find ever greater musical fame, but I will remain at her side until she concludes her search and I reach my destination."

"Ah, Johannes, selfish as ever! Always stubborn, inflexible! So be it. But you will not win. That pleasure will be mine." And he disappeared.

The next day I hardly spoke, unable to forget what had happened in the night. In the studio, I could not concentrate. My mood had barely changed the following day when Olfert returned to our lodgings from an early-morning drawing session *en plein air* bringing reports that there had been an outbreak of the pox on the other side of the river. Shortly afterwards, we received a message from Herr Griebel urging us to join the ducal entourage leaving the city for a safer destination. While Khadra and Olfert packed the few possessions we had acquired, I hurried to the workshop to gather up our small collection of paintings. As I wrapped them in oilcloth, I noticed Gysbert's portrait of Khadra on an easel in the corner. Though it still required some fine finishing touches, I feared that in the hurry to escape the city he may have left it behind. To ensure its safekeeping, I placed the portrait with my own canvases in a handcart and set off to find my two companions. The guards rebuffed us at the palace gates but Griebel saw us and put us and our possessions in a modest carriage at the end of the ducal convoy. It was late in the day when we finally departed the palace, proceeding north-east, so the coachman told me.

In the early evening, we reached a small town where the horses were rested before we continued our journey. As we did so, it began to snow and soon the convoy slowed, effortfully making its way through a forest in worsening conditions. After a while, we had to stop for the coachman to repair one of the wheels of our carriage, then we once more picked our way through the deepening snow. When we stopped at dawn in a village on the edge of the forest there was no sign of the convoy. We had become separated. Khadra and Olfert sought warmth inside one of the cottages, while I helped the coachman clear a way for our carriage to reach the nearby highway. As I was straightening my back, a bird rested on my shovel. It looked at me.

"Hard work, is it not, Johannes? But this is what you wanted, isn't it – you and the woman still together? Well, you have your wish – for now."

I did not reply.

"And the next stop on this tortuous journey? Ah, I thought so! The commission! So much for helping her find her mother! What humbug."

I flung a handful of snow at the bird as it flew away.

Pathway cleared, we resumed our journey, arriving several hours later at the city of Jacob Hendricks. Approaching its outskirts, we passed an old man on the side of the road, walking in the opposite direction. He turned to look at us. For a moment, I thought I saw the anguished face of Khalid.

I sent a message to Hendricks soon after our arrival, asking if the guild council had chosen an artist. I received word early the next day that they had someone in mind, but would make their final decision in a week's time. I was welcome to submit examples of my work if I wished to be considered. But I should hurry.

I went to bed that night still uncertain what to do. I had been an artist for most of my life, developing a style in portraiture, occasional street scenes and, even less frequently, landscapes that might appeal to a clientele of up-and-coming merchants and their families seeking to better, and demonstrate, their social status. For many shopkeepers, farmers and those who worked in cities, a picture of their family was often beyond their means. Yet if their financial or social status changed, an early way of marking their advancement was to commission – despite still fairly modest resources – family portraits to hang on the walls of their houses. For many years, I had offered my services as an itinerant portraitist at a price acceptable to such aspiring nouveaux riches. A moderate number had accepted. In contrast, wealthier patrons, keen to flaunt more ostentatiously their greater affluence, sought to commission better known, more expensive and fashionable painters to immortalise them. I had long desired, as did many other artists, to paint a work that would hang in a more public and prestigious place and thus earn wider acclamation and, as a consequence of fame, more rewarding instructions. Now I had the opportunity to achieve such a step, thanks to a guild anxious to play a more significant role in the community. On the other hand, there was the risk that I might fail to produce a work of the scale and quality required, or that I would not be awarded the commission, and thus be condemned to remain an artist of only limited reputation and skill. I lay awake unable to decide.

The next morning Olfert hired a small conveyance to take me and the pictures to the guildhall. He was touchingly confident that I would prevail and that before long I would become a famous painter. Unwilling to disappoint him and despite my misgivings, I agreed to go.

I waited in the anteroom for Hendricks' arrival. Several times I rose to leave but the clerk assured me that, though the councillor was a busy man, he would eventually come. After over an hour had passed, I decided, despite the clerk's protestations, that I should abandon the clearly ill-starred venture, return to our lodgings and face Olfert's disappointment. As I was gathering up the paintings, Hendricks arrived.

"Come with me," he said gruffly.

I complied.

In the council chamber, he instructed me to place the pictures on the table. I did so, including Khadra's portrait.

Obviously in a hurry, he asked if all of them were mine.

"Yes," I replied, "though Olfert, whom you may recall meeting earlier, helped with the preparation of several, setting the outline and mixing the colours for my palette."

Hendricks made no further comment while he examined each work closely.

"I wish to retain these for the rest of the council to see. You must understand the judgement is the council's as a whole, not mine alone. Return in a week's time for the answer. Is that understood?"

"Yes."

"Good. Then I bid you good morning, Johannes."

I returned to our lodgings, for which Khadra was paying, from money received for several concerts she had given under the Duke's patronage. We chose not to speak about the commission. The weather turned bitterly cold.

A week later I returned to the guildhall. I waited as before in the council chamber anteroom. I could hear the murmur of voices. Almost an hour had elapsed when the door opened and Hendricks beckoned me to enter. The council members sat around the long table, some leaning upon it, others slouched in their high-backed chairs. The paintings I had brought a week ago were scattered down its length, but Khadra's portrait had been placed on an easel in the centre of the room. Hendricks assumed the role of spokesman.

"Johannes," he said, "your paintings are pleasing to the eye and in our opinion display considerable skill in execution. We are particularly impressed by your portrait of Mistress Cecilia, or

Khadra as I understand you prefer to call her. It shows a fine hand and delicacy of colour, particularly in the reflection of the candlelight upon the folds of her gown and in the rendering of her gentle face. On the basis of the work you have submitted, we have decided to award you the commission.

"But we have changed our minds as to what we wish you to paint. Instead of one painting, we wish to be ambitious and have two. The first, as originally planned, is a painting to hang in this chamber, of the present council sitting around this table, showing how upright, law-abiding and charitable we are. The second will hang above the high altar in our cathedral, in place of the current work, which is now damaged and in poor condition. Moreover, we have decided that the altarpiece should depict the Virgin and Child. We are so taken by your portrait of Mistress Cecilia that we wish her, seated, to be the model for the Virgin, of course holding the future Messiah, not her lute.

"As both paintings are required without delay, we have decided to award the commission for the painting of the council to your opponent and to appoint you as the artist of the altarpiece. The substantial amount we agreed to set aside for one grand picture will thus be split between two artists. However, whoever finishes first will receive an additional payment. Are our terms acceptable?" Hendricks looked at me hard.

I hesitated. The award to me of the commission for the altarpiece had, it would seem, been largely made on the basis of the quality of the painting of Khadra. Yet I had failed to tell them, despite ample opportunity, I was not the artist. By agreeing to their proposal, I was committing a devious, unpardonable subterfuge. But the sum of money I would receive was considerable and if, with Olfert's assistance, I worked quickly, I might be the first to finish and therefore earn the additional prize.

"Well, Johannes, what is your answer? We have not got all day!"

"I accept," I replied.

"Good. Then everything is settled. You will begin work within the month. Let us know as soon as possible what materials and facilities you will need and we will find you suitable lodgings at our expense, preferably close to the cathedral. They will be modest but sufficient for your purposes."

The clerk showed me out.

I walked through the city, ashamed of what I had done. But there was no going back. I had given my word to the guild. Though my return to the north – to my home – was still not completed, and Khadra's mother was still unidentified and unfound, I wanted to seize this chance, albeit based on deception, to try to paint a masterpiece and so become a celebrated artist with wealthy clients knocking at my door. The price would be having to stay, being unable to fulfil my promise to Khadra or to ease my troubled spirit. False pride and dishonesty had intervened.

I heard a familiar voice.

"So, Johannes, at last you have done what I foretold would happen. You and Mistress Khadra will go your separate ways. Your pride and ambition have triumphed over your promise to her. So much for your high-minded moralising."

CHAPTER NINE

Into the Long Night

In the ensuing month, the existing painting above the high altar was prepared for removal and, before long, it was taken away. I visited the cathedral daily to view the immensity of the void it had left and to visualise how my painting would fill it. Each evening I stood before the altar, it seemed the dark space had become even greater, my task ever more daunting. I imagined what it must have been like for those ancient sea captains who, the night before they set sail, by flickering candlelight, studied their charts and books once again, almost overcome by the huge challenge before them – to sail across unmapped oceans of unknown extent to discover unproved territories in the New World and claim ownership for the greater glory of their royal patrons.

So it was for me. I was about to embark, in self-inflicted isolation, on a voyage across a boundless ocean of patience and endeavour to create a masterpiece – still just a figment of my imagination – of great proportions, not only to satisfy the self-indulgent pride of my patrons but also to satiate my own hunger for praise. There would be no ports of call, no fair wind. Like the voyagers of discovery, I was embarking on a journey from which there could be no turning back. To do so would bring shame, ridicule and dismissal without recompense, whereas completion would deliver respect and renown. Nothing would matter except to savour the triumph of success over failure. My stubbornness would push me forward against all odds but I would voyage alone – no companionship, no comfort. Yet was I destined to succeed or was I approaching ambition's graveyard?

Despite the council's offer to find me lodgings, I decided to work and live in the cathedral sacristy, in order to safeguard the secrecy of my composition. Grateful to avoid any expense, however modest, they readily agreed, wasting no time in arranging the removal to one of the other sacristies the hangings and linens usually kept there, so that the church might continue its holy business undisturbed by my unorthodox presence.

I had barely begun to prepare my *modello* – my oil sketch on paper – of the central composition of the altarpiece, which would portray the Virgin and her Child surrounded by saints and a heavenly host proclaiming her divinity, when Hendricks came to inform me that the councillors wished to appear in the picture in place of the holy and celestial figures. I protested. Though mindful they had commissioned me to paint the altarpiece, I argued that such a portrayal would be inappropriate, indeed some might claim blasphemous. In medieval depictions, I insisted, only saints and angels were portrayed in close proximity to the divine. Surely the other commission, by the artist whose identity I still did not know, would fulfil their need for recognition of their good works? Hendricks was at first unpersuaded but, after conveying my strong opinion to the council, he returned to say that I should proceed as I intended but that, as a compromise, the coats of arms of the council members should be displayed in the painting. I reluctantly agreed and begged him not to intervene again.

As I switched my efforts to the plain-weave prepared canvas – placing it on a fixed wooden stretcher for destubbing and then wetting, followed by restretching, a process I laboriously repeated three times to ensure the canvas's tension – I began to consider what background I should add to the painting. Should it be European, as the council would expect, or reminiscent of the East? In the silent and sombre sacristy, I could never erase from my mind the sights and sounds of Palestine – the heat, the cold, the dust, the colour, the mysterious figures in their keffiyehs, the camels. The daily chants and prayers in the cathedral were muted by the mesmerising and evocative sound in my head of the oud and other instruments I had heard on our way to Jerusalem. I imagined the

Virgin on her journey to Bethlehem riding not a donkey but a camel, swaying gently as it conveyed her to be counted in the emperor's census, a veil shielding all but her eyes from the dust and concealing her unknowable thoughts while an abaya swathed her body and hid the Child she was carrying. Reflecting on all I had seen in Palestine – recollections I could not put aside however hard I tried – I decided that the background to her portrayal would include horses, camels and elephants, which the magi surely would have ridden as they made their way to the town with their gifts.

The Virgin posed the greatest challenge for my brush. The council had stated that Khadra should be her model, that I should present her just as Gysbert had done, in a sitting position. In his portrait, she was young, striking, confident, poised and simply dressed. The Virgin in my depiction would indeed be Khadra – young, striking and poised – but expressed differently. I would portray her standing, bathed in an emerging light, dressed in a silken gown of the richest blue, open at the front to reveal an undergown, crimson in colour with a boat-shaped neckline, much like the undergarment I had seen her wear so boldly in Jerusalem. The hood of the outer robe would be slipping from her head, thus freeing her long flowing hair to cascade around her shoulders. The shadows in the painting's background would contrast with the Virgin's lighter skin, drawing the eyes of those who gazed at the altarpiece directly to her face, which, looking openly straight at them, would reflect not only pride of motherhood and beauty but also vulnerability and bewilderment at what she already knew would happen to the Child in her arms. The Child Himself would not evince confidence but have an imploring expression, as Olfert had shown as he looked up at us before climbing onto the elephant's back when we departed from Venice.

Behind the Virgin, towards the foot of the painting and in the middle distance, would be a stone-pillared structure of archways bearing the coats of arms of the council members, so displaying civil power, and through the arches, in the far distance, would be a mighty castle to convey military power. Within its great height and breadth the altarpiece would also contain, in a small detail, a foreshadowing of the crucifixion: through one of the arches, on the horizon, I would paint three crosses, resembling the gruesome gallows Khadra, Olfert and I had seen as we navigated the river on our way to the castle of curiosities.

Looking at my *modello* I already knew that the altarpiece, as I had sketched it, in considerable detail, on paper and which I would now replicate on canvas in a long and painstaking process, was not in accordance with what Hendricks and his fellow councillors were expecting. But no matter. Inspired by Khadra I was determined not only to recapture what I had seen in Palestine but also to present what I imagined the Virgin had seen and experienced on her own journey of discovery and, later, sorrow. For me, this composition would be an inspiring and elevated form of art.

In the early days of the canvas's further preparation, particularly in its sizing using rabbit-skin glue, Olfert came each morning with food and fresh materials. When I heard him at the sacristy door I covered the *modello* so he would not see it. He often entreated me to show him what I had drawn but I steadfastly refused. After a short stay, he would leave, promising to return the next day. At night, I often worked by candlelight until, in my fatigue, I could no longer stand. My sleep was erratic and in the darkness of the small hours I frequently heard the distant voice of my tormentor, challenging my determination and skill, or, if not him, the sniggering voices of demons stepping down from their lofty gargoyle positions to run amok in the nave.

Eventually, the day came when the canvas was placed onto its final stretcher, reinforced by cross batons with wooden keys inserted, so that I could adjust it to allow for movement of the canvas. Olfert helped me to begin the next stage – the application to the canvas of a base of chalk and oil, followed by another protective coat. When that had been completed, he assisted me in applying a priming layer of linseed oil, lead white and charcoal slack, which would give the painting the tonality I sought. This long and laborious process took several weeks. At the same time, he and I began to mix and experiment with the pigments I would require. Throughout this period I refined my *modello*, which Olfert pestered me incessantly to reveal, as did Hendricks. But I continued to refuse. I wanted no one to see my creation until it was unveiled above the high altar.

Many weeks had passed without my seeing Khadra. Instead, she would send me messages, through Olfert, telling me of her musical progress. I had encouraged her, following the veiled woman's visitation, to write her own music, and her news included word of her first compositions for the lute and harpsichord, an instrument she had begun to play at the suggestion of her friend, Madame Marie-Thérèse, with whom she and Olfert were spending their days.

Within three months, the canvas had been smoothed, sized and finally prepared with a ground and priming, and the *modello* was done. The canvas confronting me, on its final stretcher, was twice the size I had originally planned, and would fill the entire space from the altar to the roof of the apse. I knew that my remaining work, to transform the image in my *modello* to fulfilment in oil, would last neither many weeks nor many months but a year or even longer. Hendricks paid one of his regular visits to learn of my headway. When he realised that the task would be lengthy, he warned that the council were impatient. Having awarded the commission they were keen to see their expectations realised: a work of great art to the glory of the guild, cathedral and city. They would find any significant delay in completion hard to justify. Were that to happen, the costs of extra paint and other materials would be defrayed against my payment, if they became exorbitant. I turned a deaf ear to his warnings. What had to be must prevail above all other considerations.

The night before I began to paint the central figure of the Virgin, Olfert left while the cathedral bell was chiming twelve and I sat down in front of the canvas, the top of which, in the darkness of the sacristy, seemed to reach into the heavens, to contemplate my task. Would the completed altarpiece be a celebration of the Virgin and Child or would it be solely an expression of Khadra's beauty? Would I have the skill to convey a woman's beauty as Gysbert had done? Would I be able to create a work of great wonderment? What had I done, imposing such a burden of expectation on my shoulders?

To add to my turmoil, earlier in the evening a letter had been pushed under the sacristy door. I read its heart-piercing words again.

Dear Johannes,

I send you my warmest greeting.

That you and I have not spoken for many weeks because of your seclusion has caused me great sadness. After all, you and I have been close companions on our long and as yet uncompleted journey to the north. Your withdrawal has shown me you are now committed to a great new enterprise, which I hope, when it is finished, will bring you long-sought ease of mind, tranquillity and satisfaction. You have taught me much and, following your wise advice, I have begun my own enterprise, in the cause of music, not only to play the compositions of others with greater skill but to write and share my own. I also seek love, as a young woman should do.

In your absence, which I have come reluctantly to accept, I have been befriended by and spent much time with the widow Marie-Thérèse. With her assistance, I will leave this city tomorrow to journey further on my own, to seek fulfilment of my ambition in a kingdom far beyond the boundaries of this one.

I will greatly miss you and your tender care but, as Olfert has told me there is no prospect of an early end to your all-consuming endeavour, I have decided this is the time for us to part. Perhaps it will be possible for us to meet again one day and, if we have not yet completed our respective journeys, once more to go forward together so that you are able to return to the place from which I took you and I might find my own solace. Though we must part, you should know I will think of you often and I hope you will do the same of me. Olfert will remain with you for a while longer until he decides his own path to follow in life.
Adieu.
Your companion, Khadra

I folded the letter and placed it back in my pocket, gazed once more at the blank canvas on which I would begin work at daybreak. I would have to complete my journey on my own.

"Ah, Johannes! What sadness! A painting to begin, to satiate your personal vanity, and your companion gone. How are you going to complete your journey to the north now?"

I turned to see the man in the smiling mask. He approached the canvas, a knife in one hand, candle in the other.

"Shall I cut the canvas to shreds, burn your *modello* and spirit you away from this place so you can join your beloved Khadra? Or shall we let her go and you can begin, alone, the monstrous, impossible task you have set yourself?"

He moved closer to the canvas, raising the knife ready to strike. I lunged at him.

"No, no, no! Let her go. Leave the canvas unblemished, the drawing intact! I have made my choice and I will live with the consequences. I will bear them, however hard that may prove, because nothing will deflect me from completing my task. I will prove you wrong, hideous tormentor, as I have done already. I will finish this painting and then resume my journey to the north. I damn you for all eternity, whoever you are. Leave my sight!"

He slowly placed the knife back in his belt, the candle on the table, and nonchalantly patted my shoulder.

"So be it," he whispered in my ear. "But I'm sure I will be back. Have no doubt of that, Johannes!"

With that, he vanished into the darkness, the hem of his cloak extinguishing the candle as he did so. And thus, like the captain of a ship embarking the next morning for the unknown, I lay down in darkness, exhausted, fearful but yet with a small measure of exhilaration. Before long the first rays of daylight would begin to penetrate the high sacristy window, and thereafter my voyage would begin, without my young companion.

The next morning, I applied the first stroke of my brush. I had already decided that, from then on, neither Olfert nor Hendricks nor any priest would be permitted to enter the sacristy. Food and materials would be left outside the locked door. No one would glimpse the genesis and evolution of my creation. As winter set in, the unceasing cold penetrated my bones and made the paint slow to dry. But, slowly, the image of the Virgin began to emerge from the canvas.

CHAPTER TEN

The Echo of Music

In the candlelight, I stepped back to gaze at the canvas, my eyes heavy with fatigue. The paint I had applied made its dimensions seem even greater, dwarfing the sacristy. I could not say how many weeks – perhaps even months – had passed since the first stroke of my brush. I began each day in the early light of dawn and often continued long after dark with an array of candles to illuminate each painstaking application from my palette. I had quickly become oblivious to the world beyond the walls behind which I had hidden myself. My routine was as fixed, elemental and relentless as the movement of the planets or the tides.

Now, the Virgin – Khadra – was almost complete. She smiled. More paint had yet to be applied to add lustre to her face and to give more tone and contrast to her hair and richness to her gown and undergarment. And I had yet to add the background – the illumination of the heavens behind the Virgin, and the stone arches and crosses in the lower part of the canvas – as well as place the Christ Child in her arms. I glanced at Gysbert's painting of Khadra and then at my own depiction. His portrait was graceful, a true reflection of her beauty. But mine, I convinced myself, had greater depth, insight and humanity. As I had told Hendricks during his most recent interrogation of my progress – conducted outside the sacristy, in accordance with my resolution that no one should enter – I was now more than halfway towards the fulfilment of the council's commission. I added that, whilst waiting over the past weeks for each layer of paint to dry, I had worked feverishly to complete two smaller panels, which I had decided to add to my commission, to hang eventually on either side of the altarpiece. The first panel portrayed the magi arriving in Bethlehem, on camel, elephant and horse, while the other bore the images of Olfert as John the Baptist and Maddalena as his mother Elizabeth, recapturing the poignant scene on our departure from Venice.

All those life-suspending weeks before, when I submitted the samples to the guild then accepted the commission, I had begun my descent into the deep pit of hell – a place Dante had vividly described in *Inferno*, within his *Divine Comedy* – branding myself as a perjurer, a deceiver, a manipulator, a lost soul. Now my half-finished creation stood before me. Might what I was creating be the beginning of my redemption? I drank more wine and lay down on my bed. There was no sound from the cathedral but in the far distance I could hear music and occasional laughter and applause. I extinguished the last candle to begin my drift towards sleep. Then came the voice of my tormentor. He sat beside my bed, a candle in his hand, its light illuminating his grotesque mask.

"I have been watching you, Johannes. I commend your skill, master painter. Your stubbornness has borne fruit. Of course, you still have much more to do and in due course you will have to confess to Hendricks that you have deviated from your commission. But I imagine you will argue that such a step is artistic licence and brush aside his remonstrations."

I cursed him. "Leave me be! I am the maker of my destiny, not you. I will achieve what I have decided to do. I will not allow you to deflect me. Get out!"

"Why should I do that? I thought we were friends. After all, we dined together in Venice and we've spoken many times since then. You and I are inseparable companions – in contrast to you and Khadra."

"Khadra is not your concern. And you and I are not inseparable companions, as you put it. I did not invite you to dine with me in Venice. You were an insufferable intrusion. I wish to have no truck with you. I will do as I please. I'm not in thrall to you. I will finish the altarpiece and then I will seek to complete my journey to the north."

He did not reply. He merely smiled, his mask conveying

bonhomie and malice in equal measure. His taunting resumed.

"Do you not think of her? Do you not sometimes wonder what has happened to your erstwhile companion? Judging by the image you have painted you are clearly reminded of her every day. It must be painful for you to think of others enjoying her company and the pleasure of her music, being aroused by her beauty."

I looked at him, his mask now more hideous than ever, trying to think of words that might pierce his armour.

He persisted. "Don't tell me you have become so absorbed in your commission that you have not pondered her fate?"

I still did not answer.

"For heaven's sake, man. The Virgin you have painted is Khadra, not some divine inspiration. You are obsessed by her." He dragged me from the bed and, putting his hand around my neck, thrust me close to the picture. "As you created those eyes, her lips, her hair, surely you must have been racked by jealousy that such a beautiful woman might be adored and lionised by others, playing her music to them, not you, while you have locked yourself in this room for weeks, months, seeking to recreate on canvas a woman only you can possess?"

In reply I stumbled, trying to free myself from his iron grip. He let go and pushed me back onto the bed.

"Come, Johannes, speak! You have a tongue."

"As I paint, Khadra is here with me – on the canvas. I am able to talk to her. That is sufficient. I do not need to know what she might be doing."

He sat down beside me, putting an arm around my shoulder in a gesture far from comforting.

"Johannes, listen! Do you hear that music?"

"Yes, I hear it."

"That is your beloved Khadra, or Cecilia as she is known in the country in which she now resides. She is about to play to His Majesty the King. She performs often at his court. She is admired by all, envied by many, lusted after by the countless eager to bed her."

The music became louder.

"You may say so. But for me, Khadra is here, in my painting. Real and present enough."

"Johannes, let us go to see her."

"No. I will not leave this sacristy until the altarpiece is completed."

"Johannes, I know you do not want to leave. And it is not for me to drag you from here against your will in the dead of night. I could, of course, but I don't think that is necessary. Just look at Khadra as you have painted her and then close your eyes."

I tried to resist but it proved impossible, his fingers once again tight around my neck. As I looked at the canvas, the room was suddenly filled with light, the sound of people talking and laughing.

"Johannes, close your eyes!"

"Pray silence for His Majesty."

The gilded room, illuminated by dozens of candles, fell quiet as the King took his place, surrounded by lavishly dressed courtiers – dukes, duchesses, marquises, marchionesses, lords, mistresses.

"Be seated," commanded the King. "Tonight we will be entertained by a new musician from Venice and further east. She has come on the recommendation of our illustrious and much-esteemed court composer, Madame Élisabeth Jacquet de la Guerre and, of course, the Queen." The King signalled for the door to the chamber to be opened.

Khadra entered, carrying her lute, followed by the King's orchestra. She stood before the monarch, curtsied, then stepped onto a low dais and took her seat. She wore a deep-red silk dress, décolleté, full-skirted and with elbow-length sleeves slashed to reveal white silk beneath. Her hair was pinned up but without adornment, contrary to the prevailing style at court. The King looked at her intently.

"Mademoiselle, I understand from Madame Jacquet that you will start with music you have composed yourself."

"Sire, that is so."

"Then please begin."

Accompanied by two violins and harpsichord, Khadra began to play a sonata with four movements. The court sat spellbound by her virtuosity and fluency, and the expressive eloquence of her lute's dialogue with the violins.

"Brava, mademoiselle," said the King. "Will you not play us something more?"

"If it be your wish, sire," Khadra replied. "This is another composition – *Fantasia Prima* – of which Madame Jacquet has approved."

"Mademoiselle, it is I who will approve. Please play and let me judge."

Khadra inclined her head, acknowledging the mild rebuke, compliant, while the faintest of smiles hinted at confidence in a favourable verdict. She began playing alone, her fingers plucking the strings to create a gentle melody that ebbed and flowed in spirit. Then, towards the end, she beckoned the orchestra to join her in a concerto I had once heard her play at the *seminario*, though at the time I did not know it was a piece she had composed.

Gentle applause from the still hushed, rapt audience rippled through the chamber when she had finished.

"Mademoiselle Cecilia, I understand that you sing, too. Is that the case? If so, before my principal court composer dislodges you from the dais – worried for his position, perhaps – we would be honoured to hear your voice. What will you sing for us?"

"It is called *Laudate Dominum*, Your Majesty."

"Please proceed, despite this fellow's unworthy impatience."

Khadra began to sing, her words, gypsy-like and in Arabic, harmonising with the swaying tune she played on her lute, the body of which she struck to emphasise the beat. Two violins accompanied her. Her voice was dextrous and supple, as I recalled from her singing long ago on the voyage to Palestine. The King sat amazed, whether by her voice or her beauty was hard to say.

"Brava, mademoiselle. You must play for us more often. Madame Jacquet has advised you well."

As the principal court composer eagerly took his place on the dais, younger courtiers gathered around Khadra. Her notable admirer was Lord de la Roche, introduced to her by the Queen.

*

"See, Johannes," my tormentor whispered, "what a triumph she proved. And the way she spoke to the King – coquettish, I would say. He could not take his eyes away from her. See what you're missing – locked up in these miserable surroundings. If you had accompanied her, you might now be living in comfort at court, by Khadra's side."

"What you showed me was an illusion, a trick, a figment of your insidious, malevolent imagination. I am content to be here, completing my commission."

"Johannes, you are always in denial. Would I trick you?"

With that he disappeared.

Still heedless of the passage of time beyond the sacristy, I pressed on with my task. But as I put the final touches to the Virgin and her Child and began to focus on the background to the altarpiece, I could not erase from my mind the recollection of Khadra at court. Every day, every hour, the music I had heard her play rang in my ears, while the colour of her dress, her poise and her beauty were images I could not escape. I struggled with the impulse to begin the canvas again, to paint an even fairer portrait. Despite these distractions, the picture progressed.

Late one evening, following yet another remonstration from Hendricks, I stood back and looked at the almost completed canvas, the day's accents of paint still wet. Within the next week, the frames would arrive into which I would place the finished work. And a week after that, the picture and side panels would be removed and placed above the high altar. My task would be done. It would then be for Hendricks, the council and the city to see the completed commission. It would be a day of judgement.

As I rested, greatly fatigued, I heard the locked sacristy door rattle. It was my tormentor, entering without a key.

"Well, Johannes, I had to return to see the finished product – close up, you might say." He stood before the canvas. "I must admit, your work is truly impressive. Of course, I'm not usually interested in altarpieces. I leave such matters to others. But I misjudged you, Johannes. I misjudged your willpower, your commitment, your stubbornness to complete the task. Yet, at what a cost! Khadra gone, Olfert gone, only you and the painting left, and soon you will be parted even from that. And what will Hendricks and his fellow councillors say when they see how far you have deviated from your commission? I look forward to seeing their faces at the unveiling and to your reaction."

"I do not care what they say. My commission will be complete."

"And if they decide not to pay you? What will you do then? Have you thought of that?"

"Whatever they may say and decide – good or bad, payment or not – I will have done what I set out to do."

"And then what?"

"I will resume my journey to the north."

"It will be unaccompanied, Johannes. Remember, no Khadra and no Olfert. You will be alone."

In the distance, I heard the echo of a woman's laughter.

"That's Khadra," said the man in the smiling mask.

"What of her?" I shrugged.

"There is more of her to tell."

"I don't wish to know."

"But you should. After all, she was your companion."

"But no longer. I wish her well."

"Come, Johannes, one last look. Let's see how fortune has served her."

"I repeat, I do not wish to know."

"And I say again that you should know. You should see Khadra now so you can decide whether you made the right choice – to remain here rather than enjoying her companionship. Johannes. I want you to see so you can judge whether you were right or wrong in your decision."

"I can't. I won't."

"Come, Johannes, let us go. After all, am I not your conscience?" Standing in front of the canvas he gripped my arm tightly. "Look intently at her, Johannes."

It was an early sunlit morning. I stood close to a beautiful garden, full of spring flowers. Nearby was an ancient church, a short distance from the King's palace. Inside, two people knelt before the altar, a man and a veiled woman. A priest stood in front of them, performing the rite of marriage before a small congregation. From amidst the grotesque gargoyles and the saints with fixed, expressionless faces I looked down towards the altar, a distant, helpless witness.

As the couple, now husband and wife, turned towards the congregation and bowed to the King, I wept to see my beloved Khadra, no longer my companion, one in memory only. Later that day, in the garden, I watched as the two walked ahead of me, arm in arm, oblivious to the world around them. They kissed. Unable to escape the pain of what my tormentor was forcing me to observe, I saw them again in the evening when they drew the curtains around their bed to enter their own private world of love and submission. The following day I watched as she descended the staircase in the palace. She saw me and smiled.

"Johannes, my dear friend, what are you doing here? It is indeed a pleasure to see you again after such a long time. What became of you? You were so obsessed with your own preoccupations, never joining me in the evenings, that I concluded you had forgotten me, that you no longer wanted to continue our journey north. You never replied to my letter informing you of my decision to leave without you. You never came to say goodbye. So, though I waited until the last moment in the hope you would appear, I left to continue my journey alone. Now I have found happiness, though sadly the question of who my mother is remains unanswered. As for you and me, our journey together is over. I am in love, married, and I will continue to play music and to compose more. And I have found Agneta – or rather, she found me. She escaped the castle fire, unharmed, thank the merciful heavens, and her wanderings in search of peace and nature's gifts brought her to this city. My dear husband has provided the two of us with a walled garden, almost identical to the one in the castle she nurtured and cherished. There we sit and talk and often I play the lute to her as she sketches and paints. I consider her the loving mother I never had.

"So, Johannes, this is the end of our companionship, yours and mine, though I take with me happy memories of our adventure together and of your great kindness. Now I am afraid you must go. If you do not, you will be arrested by the guards as a trespasser. There is nothing for you here. You must complete your journey on your own."

She took my hand in hers and gently kissed it – the first time her lips had touched my skin.

"Goodbye, Johannes. I will never forget you."

With those words, she turned. I watched as she walked away, her beloved lute slung across her back.

"She's gone, Johannes." The masked man's voice brought me, bereft, back to the sacristy. "All you have is your portrait of her and it is not even yours. It will hang above the high altar, out of reach and shared by others. As for Gysbert's portrait of her, what will you do? Give it back, or destroy it?"

His words and Khadra's parting – it felt as though my heart had been pierced by a sword. I could not reply, so pained was I.

"Your only option, Johannes, once the picture has been taken to the high altar, hung and unveiled, is to leave this city. You will have no choice but to continue your journey to the north – without Olfert and, of course, without Khadra, now an acclaimed young musician and composer at the King's court. You cannot stay here, if you are to be true to yourself. It will be hard to journey alone but you're a practical man. I'm sure you will survive. And of course, you will not be completely alone. I forgot to say that you will still have me as a companion. I won't let you down." He laughed.

I seized the knife from his belt, not to kill him, much as I wished him gone, but to plunge the blade into the canvas. He gripped my wrist.

"No, Johannes, do not allow your morbid sorrow to destroy what you have created. To do that will be akin to plunging the knife into your heart. Have the courage to let others judge the quality of your art. You have a journey to complete. But before you leave, before this picture can be unveiled, there is a small blank space left here on the canvas. You must decide how it should be filled. Don't let another artist complete it for you."

"There is no more to be done! I have finished."

"Don't wallow in self-pity, Johannes. Do what you have to do. If you don't, I will turn into a raven again and place myself there. How about that? A smiling raven greeting the Virgin and our Lord."

"No! You will not!"

"Then paint, Johannes, paint what you know should be there – a distinctive mark to remind those who look at the painting of you the artist. I will return before the week is out to see that you have done so."

True to his word, he did, and nodded, satisfied.

Early the following week the great frame arrived, together with the smaller frames for the two side panels, gold but not elaborately carved, the overall effect one of simplicity, to offset the portrait not overwhelm it. Three days later the canvases had been inserted and the altarpiece was complete. That evening I sat for many hours gazing at the figure of the Virgin, remembering Khadra in Jerusalem and as I had seen her at her marriage.

Stirring from deep sleep, I heard the bell strike three o'clock in the morning. I lit a candle to look once more at my creation. Suddenly, the image came alive, the sacristy filled with light, sound and colour, the air thick with different fragrances. From every corner of the receding darkness emerged throngs of Arabs, Jews, Armenians and Ottomans – just as I had seen them in Jerusalem during my search for Khadra – playing tambourines, sackbuts and drums, their sandaled feet tapping to the syncopated beat of their eastern melody. Amongst the musicians I saw Abd al Bari, the cloth merchant, joyfully banging a tambourine on his thigh. Behind came scores of camels, horses and elephants, swaying and prancing to the same insistent and beguiling rhythm. Khadra emerged from amongst the mêlée, energetic, confident and striking, a smiling child, the infant Olfert, in her left arm, clinging tightly to her. As she approached, her hips moved in time to the music, her right arm raised above her head, fingers clicking to the beat. Her face beaming in joy, she drew closer. Reaching out, she clasped my hand in hers and, despite considerable diffidence on my part, we began to dance – hip to hip, face to face – to the lively, intoxicating music.

"Faster, Johannes, faster!" Khadra urged.

Never had I danced such steps. We reeled in an ever-frenzied spin, laughing, breathless, ecstatic, without a care. Then, when it seemed we might whirl into space, the music eased in pace and volume, gradually slowing until it became inaudible, the room once more plunged into darkness and silence. Still trying to catch my breath and still dizzy, I held the candle close to the painting. The camels, horses and elephants were once more just painted images, as I had portrayed them. The Virgin was motionless but smiling, just as I had depicted her, except that I detected an added twinkle in her eye.

"Oh Khadra. How I miss you!"

I fell to my knees, unable to contain my sense of loss. Sobbing, I fell asleep.

The next morning, I fastened the red velvet shroud, which Hendricks had provided, around my creation. My commission was complete.

CHAPTER ELEVEN

Procession and Revelation

I heard it plainly.

"All clear!" came the cry, its echo rippling down the long, dark nave. As the great bell in the towering spire rang the midnight hour, the heavy doors of the cathedral were slammed shut and the bolts driven home. The sound – its finality – was unmistakable, ricocheting from pillar to pillar.

"All secure!" came the second cry. There was silence. Then a fist pounded on the sacristy door.

"Johannes, the time has come. Open up." Hendricks' voice.

This was the moment. There was no turning back. I looked once more at the shrouded altarpiece. My hand shook as I turned the key in the lock and slowly pulled the door open. The councillor stood on the threshold, arms akimbo, dressed like an executioner in black from neck to toe, apart from his white ruff. Behind him stood eight broad-shouldered men, similarly dressed. Beyond them, flares burned in their sconces on the pillars. Hendricks gently bowed.

"Johannes, the scaffold awaits you. The iron hooks have been driven into position above the altar in accordance with your specified measurements of height and width – all exactly as you instructed. It is now time to convey your work to be hung. The great Mass to dedicate the new altarpiece is tomorrow. There is not a moment to be lost."

I nodded. After checking once again that the red velvet shroud around the painting and its side panels was firmly secure, I beckoned the eight men to lift the picture from its support and to carry it horizontally to the scaffold – four on either side, as though bearing a coffin. I followed them, Hendricks beside me.

As the procession began its slow, careful progress along the nave, from above came the distant chant of monks in the adjacent abbey, seeming to accompany my work to its place of judgement. Behind us a solitary drum beat out the pace of the pallbearers. The flares cast flickering shadows, barely penetrating the darkness that enveloped us. I heard a strange cry overhead. In the wavering light of a flare, I looked up and thought for a moment I saw a gargoyle atop a pillar turn its misshapen, greedy face to watch the cortège. As we approached the altar, the grim outline of the scaffold began to emerge from the shadows, two ropes hanging loose in readiness for the load they would bear. I shuddered. Would it be the painting or me that would hang?

At the foot of the scaffold, the pallbearers placed the altarpiece upright against the wooden framework. Pushing the bearers aside, I secured the ropes around the shroud. Then I and six of the eight men slowly mounted the scaffold. Once on its platform, I lit great candles, two either side of where the painting would hang, and directed the men to take hold of the two stout ropes, three on each.

"When I give the command, pull slowly and evenly. Do not let go. If you do, all will be lost."

Hendricks looked up, his impassive face barely visible in the gloom. Six pairs of hands adjusted their grip.

"Pull!"

The ropes tensed. The scaffold shuddered as it began to bear the added weight. Slowly, inch by inch, the painting began its ascent. Halfway, one of the men sneezed, causing his rope momentarily to slacken and the shrouded altarpiece to tip sideways.

"Pull, man! For mercy's sake, do not let go!" I cried.

The rope tightened once again and after more stressful minutes the painting finally came to rest on the scaffold. As those around me shuffled the picture – as before, inch by inch – towards the wall, I unwrapped the oilcloth bound around the thick chain affixed to the back of the centre frame. With the painting now upright and close to the wall beneath the great east window, I placed a narrow wooden box step – an executioner's block – precariously on the rear edge of the scaffold behind the painting. Then, with the weight of the painting pressing against me, I climbed the block and, with some difficulty in the darkness, hands trembling and face sweating, I managed on the fourth attempt to hook the chain onto the iron hooks driven into the wall. I tightened the chain, and when I was sure it was secure I ordered the six men beside me to let go of the altarpiece, descend to the nave and once there, on my instruction, gradually to ease the wooden structure away from the altar.

With the last man on the platform gone, I stood alone on the scaffold. The moment had come for me to say farewell to the painting on which I had toiled so long. I slowly unfolded the side panels, each individually covered, opening them out to flank the central portrait. I stepped back to take one final look at the shrouded picture, visualising the figure concealed beneath, that beautiful, vulnerable face. She would no longer be mine. Henceforth, she would belong to others, not me, worshipped by others, not me. I had deserted Khadra in life, now I was relinquishing my personal and private depiction of her. My heart felt it had suffered multiple cuts. After this moment, I would be alone. My journey north would be without her. I loosened the shroud and checked that the four white cords, which, when pulled, would remove it, were in position. Then, in a last gesture of farewell, I placed both hands on the shroud and murmured adieu, to the Virgin I had featured from the start and to the figure I had added at the end.

It was time.

"Are you ready?" I called down to the waiting men.

"Yes," came the cry from below.

The scaffold swayed as it was slowly moved away. As it crept forward, I carefully eased the weight of the massive altarpiece off its remaining lip of support into the darkness beyond the edge of the platform. I sensed a shadow beside me. I turned but no one was there. The scaffold inched still further from the wall. Suddenly, the shrouded picture lost all footing and, like the condemned man at a hanging, dropped silently into the void. My heart stopped, convinced that the chain or iron hooks would not bear the weight and that my work would crash onto the great altar below. But the drop was checked and my work fell flush against the wall, suspended from its fixtures. I waited. Still it might fall. The chain creaked gently, settling into its load. But it held.

"Johannes, how much longer will you be?" Hendricks shouted.

"I am coming!" As I uttered those words, I stepped backwards – but too far, beyond the edge of the platform. I lost my balance and fell back into the darkness. I reached out blindly. My hand struck one of the ropes used to haul up the picture. I grabbed it.

"Johannes, you may not like me but you must confess, I do have my uses. Yet another favour you owe me." I heard the familiar chuckle of the man in the smiling mask, his cold hand momentarily on mine.

Two of the men caught me as I twisted to the ground. Helped to my feet, my heartbeat slowly returning to normal and panic subsiding, I watched as the scaffold was dismantled, its spars and planks removed. Now, in the flickering light of the candles each side of the altar, the shrouded painting hung in solitary suspension. The four white cords trailed to the floor. When next they were touched, they would release the shroud and reveal my creation for all to see.

"Come with us, Johannes, and rest before the Mass tomorrow," said Hendricks. "Then we shall see whether you have fulfilled your commission or made fools of us all."

"No, I will not accompany you. I wish to remain here to keep watch – to ensure that what I have created is safe from prying eyes."

Hendricks urged me to go with them, insisting that the altarpiece would not be touched. But I was immovable. I could not bear to leave Khadra.

"So be it, my friend," replied Hendricks, turning to join the departing pallbearers.

I heard their steps fade into the darkness, the cathedral's side door close behind them and the lock turned. I was now alone. A dark shadow came silently to stand beside me.

"Well, Johannes, I take my hat off to you. It took longer than I

– and indeed you – anticipated but you've completed your task. In the morning comes the public judgement of success or failure. What a worrying time for you! And Khadra not here to give you support!"

"I do not want your companionship. I wish to stay here on my own until dawn, preparing to receive judgement. Once I've been praised or ridiculed, I will resume my journey. Until morning breaks, I wish to be alone. Do you hear that?"

"So be it, Johannes. I will leave you in this dark place. Have courage, my friend."

"I have no fear. It is said that from the darkest shadow springs the brightest light."

The man in the smiling mask departed without replying. As he did so the flares in the sconces went out one after the other as though extinguished by an unknown hand, the great candles beside the high altar likewise. I was shrouded in darkness, just like the shrouded Khadra, unseen. I lay down before her on the cold stone floor.

The nave transformed into a forest of dead trees. Shafts of faint light penetrated the leafless branches. I heard the screeching of an owl, the croaking of birds and distant muffled screams; whether they were human or animal I could not tell. I saw hunched figures running hither and thither between the tree trunks.

"Johannes, do you hear us?" came distant voices. "Remember how we used to haunt you when you were a child? How you used to call out for light but no one would hear you? You thought we had long forgotten you. We haven't, we're still here. Why don't you come and join us in the forest? The Furies are here too. You remember them, don't you, from the forest with Khadra and Olfert? Come, be with us."

"No! I will not. For pity's sake, leave me in peace!"

But they would not. The hideous noise of the forest around me became deafening. I felt a cold hand touch mine. I looked but no hand was there. Suddenly, there was a blood-curdling shriek and a giant bat flew down from a tree and lunged at me. I scrambled up and ran towards a pillar to hide from its piercing luminous eyes. It dived at me again and again. I fought it off until a blinding flash of lightning drove it and the dreadful cacophony into submission. Rain began to fall. Torrents of water poured from the black sky. Rolls of thunder pursued further flashes of lightning.

"My picture! My picture!" I screamed.

Without clear bearings, I crawled towards a distant light in the forest. Surely that was the high altar. But the light to which I crawled was a lantern outside the door of a dark, brooding house, its many shuttered windows glaring blank-eyed with each lightning strike. Drenched to the skin, I pounded on the door. It swung open. Before me was a long gloomy corridor. At the end, on the right, was a faint light. Reaching it, I found a door ajar. I pushed it open. Ahead was a large fireplace in which blazed a fire, flames devouring huge logs. Either side of the hearth were two large chairs. The room was dimly lit by candles on the walls. Between these hung mysterious, shadowy tapestries displaying grotesque animals in a forest. I heard a creak. Behind me, the door through which I had entered slowly shut; a key scraped in the lock. I turned once more towards the fire, seeking to warm my frozen hands. A faint figure, half apparition, stood before it, beckoning me. As I drew close to her, I saw she had no face. I stood rooted, unable to move. The rain, even heavier now, battered against the shutters. In the quivering light of the constant lightning flashes, I saw paintings of disfigured faces staring from the walls.

Suddenly, after a mighty clap of thunder, the storm diminished and the room became filled with a green luminescence. The locked door opened and, to escape the figure of the woman, I stepped through the doorway and found myself in a forest of huge trees, flourishing, life-filled this time, their massive trunks disappearing into the night sky. Butterflies full of light fluttered around me. The notes of strange but melodic music emanated from minute harps, suspended from verdant branches and swaying in a gentle sweet-tasting breeze. A stream trickled along the forest floor between tall white flowers, the heads of which cast upward beams of light into the sky. I walked towards a small green-walled cottage bathed in a shaft of translucent moonlight, lured by the sound of a lute. As I neared it, the door opened. The sound grew even more distinct. I hesitated and then, peering inside, I saw a child, with a beautiful smiling face, looking at me, her arms outstretched ready to receive me. But I could not move, was unable to reach her embrace. Slowly, she disappeared until there was only black emptiness. I turned away, my eyes full of tears. She had seemed such a sweet child. I walked amongst the trees, my heartache lulled by the music of thousands of harps, the whisper of the brook and the chirping of unseen birds.

Gradually, the forest too began to disappear, deeper, still soothing music, played on a multitude of pipes, replacing the sounds of before. From the darkness, there emerged a galaxy of distant stars rocking back and forth above a vast, bottomless valley. I sat on a mountain peak, consoled by the beauty of the music and bewitched by the sight of the heavens. I struggled to remain awake but felt myself steadily succumbing. I do not know how long I slept. I was wakened by the sound of an oud and distant birdsong. I saw Khadra in the distance, sitting beneath a tree, playing a gentle melody, unaware of my presence. I listened to the richness of her music echoing across the landscape. She began to walk through a grove of trees, their leaf-laden branches dipping down to touch banks of brightly coloured flowers. I followed as she skirted silent waterfalls. On she walked, never looking back. The sun rose higher in the sky.

Then came the great crashing sound of iron against wood, the tolling of a bell. Khadra turned, smiled and carried on. I tried to follow her but my body convulsed.

"Johannes, wake up." Hendricks' voice dispelled the vision in an instant. "It's morning. The revelation of the altarpiece is at noon. You must go home immediately and get ready – shave, put on fresh clothes. Be back here within two hours."

"But I must stay with my painting – to see no one unveils it before the appointed hour."

He put a reassuring hand on my shoulder.

"It will remain veiled until the commencement of Mass. The bishop will have the honour of removing the shroud, not you, not me. Now, go. There is no time to delay." He pressed some coins into my hand.

I left the cathedral. The noise of the market outside was deafening – the shouts of stallholders, the cries of customers bargaining for the best price, neighing horses, barking dogs, wheels clattering on cobbles. I passed musicians playing pipes, drums and tambourines that had barely changed since medieval times. A drunken man was dancing a jig with a toothless woman. I hitched a ride in a cart to the edge of town, gratefully leaving the din behind. I stood outside the house I had not seen for so long. A bird sang; leaves rustled. I heard a blacksmith at work in the distance. The clock struck the hour. A horse and rider galloped past. On the horizon, the sky was darkening and thunder rumbled. I peered through the keyhole. I saw a woman talking to a handsome, well-dressed man. He took her hand and kissed it. She reached for his hand in response, and held it, smiling at him. Both turned to acknowledge the presence of another. It was Olfert.

Another cart passed. I stopped it. Pressing one of Hendricks' coins into the cart driver's hand, I mounted and sat beside him.

"Which way?"

"Away from the city," I replied.

"Then I cannot help you."

"Why, which way are you going?"

"To the city market. It's market day. Surely you know that. Besides, I want to see the new altarpiece. It's to be unveiled today. So, what's it to be? Come with me or find someone else?"

Inwardly, I agonised – whether to flee from the city in cowardice or to show courage.

"Come, what is it to be? Hurry. I want to sell my corn before the market closes."

"I will go with you to the city," I replied.

The cart moved off at a rapid pace. While still overwhelmed by the urge to leave, unable to bear the public judgement of the painting, I could not bring myself to jump from the cart. Was that also cowardice, or curiosity?

Within the hour we had returned to the marketplace. The carter pulled alongside a grain merchant and began to haggle a price for his eight bags of grain. The bargaining reminded me of the way the council had set the price of my commission. I pulled my cap down lower over my face. A deal was struck and I helped empty the cart of its contents.

"Let's quench our thirst," said the cart driver. "There's an ale stall over there." I dithered. "Look, my friend. You did me a favour, unloading those sacks. Let me repay your labour with ale. Then we can go to the cathedral."

By the time we had slaked our thirst, the great west doors of the cathedral were open. The rich and famous of the city were descending from carriages and filing into the nave.

"I am not one of them," said the carter, laughing. "I'm going to enter through the abbey and look down on it all from the gallery above the nave. Come, join me."

I followed him.

Entering the abbey through its kitchen, we passed along many corridors and then climbed a steep, winding stone staircase. Reaching the top, we entered a long dark passage. The walls were decorated with crucifixes, plaques and framed images hard to see in the gloom. At the far end, a shaft of sunlight sought to penetrate the darkness. As we walked nearer, I saw the outline of a stooped figure, resting on a stick, looking out into the light. The monk half turned at the sound of our footsteps, inclined his head in gentle salutation and then shuffled forwards.

We followed him into the sunlight and onto a narrow balcony, stained-glass windows above us, each portraying a saint. Below were the serried ranks of those who had come to see the unveiling of the new altarpiece, which was still securely shrouded. To the left I could see the great west window, glorifying city heroes of the past. To the east, above the altar in the domed ceiling, was a huge hemicycle painting I had not observed before, depicting, according to the cart driver, Saxon kings of ancient times kneeling before the

Cross, their baptism by a Frankish priest symbolising their submission to the Emperor Charlemagne. I studied the faces.

"You look like that one," he whispered, pointing to the head of one of the figures to the right of the Cross. "That's Widukind – he was Charlemagne's greatest opponent during the wars between the Saxons and the Franks in the eighth century."

I looked at the kneeling figure. His weather-beaten, heavily lined face was framed by long, tousled grey hair and a heavy, unkempt beard. His eyes were hooded and he looked in suspicion and fear at the priest. I contested the carter's assertion of a likeness but he stood his ground.

"If there were to be a play in the market square about Widukind, I would choose you as the chieftain. Like him, you have a wild look about you."

A bell rang, signalling the commencement of the Mass of Dedication, and a hush descended. The congregation stood as the episcopal procession began its slow progress along the nave to the high altar, the acolytes holding huge candles, followed by priests bearing the vessels of communion and the great bible. At the rear came the bishop in his rich robes and purple cap. As they processed, the organ blasted out the notes of a grand toccata. I saw Hendricks, standing with his fellow councillors. He gazed about him, including upwards, to the balcony, seeming to seek the lowlier segments of the congregation, perhaps scanning their faces for that of the artist in whom he had placed his faith. When the procession had completed its progress and its participants had taken their places, the words rang out: "In the name of the Father, the Son and the Holy Spirit," in response to which the congregation made the sign of the cross. Thus, the Mass commenced.

The choir sang the *Kyrie*, their voices reaching every corner of the vast vaulted nave. I looked at the shrouded altarpiece, visualising the beautiful image of Khadra beneath it, shortly to be revealed. The moment of judgement was near. Then came a clarion burst from the choir as it sang *"Gloria in excelsis,"* competing in volume with the mighty organ, followed by the *Laudamus Te*. Four of the priests moved forwards, either side of the altar, to stand close to the cords which, at the bishop's signal, they would pull to reveal my work of art. I would finally be exposed for what I was.

I began to shake violently, suffocating, gasping for air. Pushing aside those around me, I stumbled back towards the passage. The words of the *Laudamus Te* followed me, ringing in my ears. I reached the top of the staircase. The music still pursued me as I half ran, half tumbled down the steps, scattering any who had the misfortune to encounter me – a demented man running from an unknown fate. I turned frantically this way and that in the complex of corridors. Finally, I reached the kitchen.

"What on earth is the matter?" asked a cook. "You look as though you have seen the devil himself."

"I must escape!"

"From what?"

"From shame!" I shouted.

As I ran towards the doorway and daylight, I heard the organ and choir reaching new soaring heights, as they sang the words *"Qui tollis peccata mundi"*. In the cobbled yard, I fell to my knees.

"Forgive me, Father, forgive my sins!" I wept inconsolably. Still the music rang in my head.

"What is the matter, sir? Let me help you," offered a yard boy, taking my arm and raising me to my feet.

"No one can help me. I am lost." I struggled to break free of his grip. "Can you hear that music – the organ and the choir?"

"I can hear nothing," he replied.

"You must be deaf, boy. The sound is ringing in my ears and all around me. I cannot escape it."

"I can hear nothing," the boy repeated. "Please, sir, wait. I will summon the monks to assist you."

"No, I do not want assistance. I cannot return inside."

As he tried to steady me, I heard the *Cum Sancto Spiritu*.

"Can you not hear that?"

Suddenly, a cloaked and hooded figure appeared at my side.

"Boy, let go. I will take care of him. He is suffering a fit of madness."

As the man in the smiling mask bore me in his arms from the

abbey, the music faded.

"Poor Johannes, your courage crumbled. You could not stay to hear the judgement of your peers. At this moment, as the *Sanctus* rings out, the shroud is slowly slipping to reveal your painting of the Virgin – or perhaps, should I say, your image of Khadra. Shall I tell you the verdict?"

"No. I beg you not to tell me."

"So be it. I will not. But is your insistence on not knowing because you think your altarpiece unworthy of its place above the high altar? Or because you fear that those who will gaze at it will see not a depiction of the Virgin but the likeness of a woman in whose company you travelled and whom you selfishly cannot bear to share?"

"I cannot say."

My bearer laughed as he put me down.

"Johannes, why do you make your life so difficult? I have offered you many opportunities to escape the toil of your endless journey of redemption, self-imposed and hard to bear. But you stubbornly persist. You test even my limitless patience."

I did not reply.

"Very well. I will accompany you to the edge of the city. There, at the inn under the sign of the Red Fox, you will find respite for the night. Tomorrow morning a stable boy will provide you with a horse on which you can begin the last part of your journey to the north. You will be alone, though I will watch you."

We walked on, each lost in our own thoughts.

CHAPTER TWELVE

The Valley of the Silhouettes

After a restless, uneasy night, I resumed my journey northwards early the following morning. I declined the stable boy's offer of a horse, deciding instead to ride with a wagoner going in the same direction. Since he was a moody fellow and I was still racked by my decision to flee the cathedral and avoid facing judgement, we spoke little to one another as his aged horse trudged along the road. Towards the end of the day, we reached a tavern called the Black Wolf. The wagoner said he intended to press on further and suggested I remain his companion, but I declined his kind offer, preferring instead to rest for the night, alone with my thoughts.

"Then be safe, my friend, on your remaining journey. Ahead are high, exposed hills and a sharp drop into the valley. I sense the weather will change tomorrow. Take care not to get caught unawares."

"I will. I don't think I'm too far from my destination."

"That may be the case, but be vigilant nonetheless. It's unfriendly land ahead. Many have got lost there, never to be seen again. That's all I will say."

He slapped me on the back as I gave him a coin or two from my near-empty purse.

The tavern was small and surprisingly busy for such an isolated place. After negotiating the price of a bed for the night, I sat down close to the fire for a simple supper of bread, cheese and ale. Nearby, a woman sat alone, a cup and teapot on the table beside her. She wore a large bonnet with ribbons à l'Alsacienne. Her dress was flounced and full-skirted with a plunging neckline, its sheen reflecting the fire. One elbow rested nonchalantly on the table, while her left hand held an opened letter. She was striking, her face bearing a slight coquettish smile as she gazed into the fire, seemingly deep in thought. There was something familiar about her which I could not place.

My attention was momentarily diverted by three travellers, noisily entering the tavern.

"Welcome!" said the taverner. "Have you come far?"

"From the city," the loudest of the three replied.

"Do you bring any titbits of gossip?" the taverner asked. "I have not been there for a while."

"Nothing salacious, but it was a big day at the cathedral two days ago – the bishop unveiled a new altarpiece. Quite the talk of the city."

"Tell me more," the taverner encouraged.

"It was a great fuss," said another of the three.

"Almost a riot," added the third.

As they moved across the room towards an empty table, I – still straining to hear more of what they were saying – became aware that the woman in the ribboned bonnet had leaned across and was speaking to me.

"You look weary and careworn. Do you live around these parts? I haven't seen you here before."

"No, I don't live in these parts. I am a traveller on a long journey, returning to the north, where I am from."

"You're alone, no companion?" she asked.

"I once had a companion but she has gone another way. So, yes, I am travelling alone. And what of you? Do you live in these parts?"

"Yes. Not far from here, in a valley."

"How far is the next town from here?"

"Not far," she replied.

She looked down at the letter resting in her lap. The same slight smile passed fleetingly across her face. She folded the letter and put it in her pocket.

"I hope it brought good news," I said, seeking distraction from gossip and thoughts of the events at the cathedral in small talk.

"Yes. I suppose it was good news – about the renewal of an old acquaintance."

We looked at each other, she smiling and me circumspect. A serving girl placed on my table the bread, cheese and ale I had ordered.

"Please join me," I offered. "It's not much but I would be happy to share it with you, madame."

Her smile deepened in amusement. "I'm not a prostitute."

"And I'm not seeking one," I replied. "As my table is closer to the fire than yours, I'm merely being hospitable."

She joined me and took a morsel of bread and cheese.

"What is your name and what is your profession?"

I mumbled, unwilling to reveal my name in case I was overheard by the three travellers still apparently relating the story of how the artist had fled from the cathedral, much to the chagrin of the council and the bishop.

"I'm an artisan, let us say."

"I am Madame Marianne."

"I'm honoured to meet you."

"When you say you're an artisan, what kind of artisan? Judging by your hands, you are not a labourer. They bear no callouses." She looked at me keenly.

"I am an artist – not a good or famed one. I paint portraits for a living."

"Would you draw me?"

"I think you deserve a better artist to capture your fine features."

"I'll be the judge of such matters." She opened her purse and took out a florin, placing it on the table. "Perhaps that will encourage you to draw me," she said.

I slid the florin back across the table as discreetly as I could, unwilling for any onlooker to think by my gesture that I was paying for her services.

"There is no need for that, madame. More to the point, I have no paper," I reasoned.

"Draw a likeness of me on the back of this." She took the letter from her pocket, unfolded it and placed it face down on the table, her delicate hands smoothing out the creases.

"But I have no means to draw."

"Johannes, judging by the dust on the cuff of your jacket you are well acquainted with red chalk. Perhaps you have a fragment in your pocket. And, while you search, I am right, aren't I? Your name is Johannes."

Taken aback, I hesitated.

"Come, is it Johannes or is it not?"

"Yes. I am Johannes."

"Now we have settled your name, please begin to draw. It should not take you long."

Retrieving an end of red chalk from my pocket, I began.

"How do you know my name?" I asked, curious and anxious in equal measure.

"I heard you were coming. People have spoken well of you and I was intrigued to meet an artist. The letter on which you are drawing described you – young, committed, talented. And a good lover, too – which, incidentally, proved to be the case."

Her words unsettled me even more. I wished she would leave.

"You must be mistaken. I am not young, as you can see, madame."

"I was talking of the past, Johannes, not the present."

As I studied her features, transcribing them onto the paper, I tried hard to remember whether and when she and I might have met. But I could not place her. She was surely mistaken. She insisted she was not.

"If we were acquainted in the past – and I do not believe we were – how long did we know each other?" I asked with trepidation.

"For a while," she replied. "Then you went away. But I could not forget you. I met another man, we married and I had a child, and then another. In the end, he too left me as, eventually, did my children."

"And now?"

"I sit and remember times past. Now, you have once more crossed my path."

I found her words increasingly disquieting.

"Better not to speak further," I said. "Let me concentrate on the task you have set me."

She nodded.

As I sketched her – my first piece of work since putting the finishing touches to the altarpiece – and she looked abstractedly at the fire, I thought about the events she had described and which I could not remember. Either my mind was befuddled or she was constructing a palpable untruth. I handed her the completed drawing.

"Thank you, Johannes. I am deeply touched. Will you come to my bed?"

Her words took me aback a second time.

"I think that would inappropriate, madame."

"Why should that be so?" she replied. "After all, we have shared a bed before. You and I are each alone this evening. So, let us enjoy the pleasure of each other – just one night, before you leave in the morning."

I sought to discourage her but she would not hear of it, her manner becoming ever more beguiling, her arguments more persuasive. Finally, she leaned across and whispered, "If you do not come, I will tell the taverner you are the artist of the altarpiece, the one who fled judgement."

"I could not bear that, madame."

"Good. Then it's agreed. You will come."

She rose from the table. I watched her as she climbed the staircase.

She lay unclothed on the bed, her limbs long and slim, her breasts shapely and firm, her unpinned hair flowing about her shoulders – a veritable artist's model. She seemed younger than the woman I had drawn downstairs, whose dress and bonnet lay discarded on the floor. She did not look up when I entered, instead remaining focused on a small object – a carving – in her fingers, turning it round and round. As I undressed in the dim candlelight, I was aware her face had become indistinct. Upon the bed, she drew me down to her, wrapping her arms tightly around me. She became quickly aroused. As I penetrated her, pulled in by her ever-stronger clasp, her nails tore at my back. For a moment I felt profound pleasure but, once she had enjoyed hers, I felt sudden sharp pain as though I had received many cuts. When she released her grip, I saw in the candle's half-light that my chest bore thorns. I began to remove them one by one. As I did so, she opened her eyes, leaned over me, a malicious smile on her almost featureless face, and whispered in my ear.

"Sweet revenge, Johannes, for what you did, for spurning me. Now sleep."

I woke in the early hours. She lay asleep beside me. Lighting the candle, I could see that my chest still bore the thorn marks. I looked at her. The contours of her limbs and body were exquisite in their shape, yet her face was still indistinct. Clutched in one hand was a small wooden figure – a Fury like the one I had seen old Greybeard, the descendant of Faustulus, carve in the forest. I tried once again to recall this woman, but still could not remember her or the earlier time she said we had been together.

A familiar spectral face, the man in the smiling mask, thrust itself through the curtains at the end of the bed.

"Well, Johannes, judging by what I observed, you certainly enjoyed the pleasure of her body, but I would deduce from the painful marks you bear that she did so more than you. Now, you have another choice to make: to relent, and become her companion, as you once were, or to leave and press on to your destination. The prospect of you reaching your destination safely without Khadra is surely doubtful. Why not make life easy for yourself and stay with the woman beside you? After all, she is a beauty – a sorceress, you might say."

"Despite your temptation, I must leave, today, to return to where this wretched and interminable journey began."

"It will be hard, Johannes. Alone – no Khadra! Let me show you how she fares."

A mist enveloped me. I stood in the middle of a beautiful palace, courtiers and servants hurrying to and fro as they prepared for a musical soirée in the presence of the King. The man in the mask put his grinning lips to my ear.

"Tonight's opera performance is Khadra's – as composer, musician and teacher. She is now the King's most highly paid courtier, in recognition of her musical virtuosity and also, I dare say, her beauty. She sings, too, as you well know from when she first lured you into the boat for Palestine, among other occasions of enchantment. She is more than a match for the King's other composers, much to their disgruntlement. And, moreover, she is married, as you saw before, and has a child. Look, Johannes, here she comes – in the King's procession."

Khadra appeared, dressed in a long white shift beneath a gold silk overgown, itself worn beneath a hip-length red jacket with white fur trimming its elbow-length sleeves and centre-front edges. Her hair was tightly pinned up.

"Your Majesty, it is my privilege to present to you this evening an opera with ballet for your delight. I have composed it in your honour – an opera showing how men can be men and women can be women, each esteeming the other in respect and harmony."

"My dear lady, please begin," said the King.

I watched an elaborate, sparkling performance of wit, romantic love and emotional intensity wrapped in exquisite music.

At the end, Khadra curtsied deeply to the King.

"I thank you greatly, my lady. You are a true rival to my principal court composer. Perhaps the time will come when you will surpass even him in achievement."

"Thank you, Your Majesty."

As the scene before me began to fade, I caught a glimpse of Khadra, her face sad and tear-stained as she sat alone singing a song of intense melancholy.

"Show me more," I pleaded. "She seems so unhappy."

"No, Johannes, I cannot."

Madame Marianne, her face now the one I had drawn, fine features again clearly delineated, stirred beside me.

"I thought I heard you speaking. To whom?"

I looked but the mask between the curtains had vanished.

"Just to myself," I replied.

"Are you leaving me?" she said.

"Yes, madame, I am leaving. I can delay no longer. I must go."

"I regret your departure. I looked forward to rekindling our love together. But if you must go, please, leave me a memento."

"I have, madame. The drawing I gave you last night."

"That is true. May I offer it back to you, Johannes, as a remembrance of me?"

"You should keep it, madame. I already have vivid memories of the past hours in my mind."

"But I require a reminder of you. Look into this mirror." She pressed a small mirror into my hand. "Johannes, look into it."

I did as she asked. My face was haggard and weary.

She took the mirror back. I dressed.

"Will you not kiss me before you go?"

I returned to the bed and leaned down towards her. As I did so, I noticed that my face was still in the mirror, which lay on the pillow. I slid it away from me. My face remained. No reflection of the bed, window or room. She smiled.

"Thank you, Johannes. I now have your portrait, too – as you are and, if you turn the mirror over towards the sunlight, you will see yourself as you once were. I will detain you no further. Au revoir."

I looked. I shuddered at my reflected images.

Leaving the tavern, on foot, I turned towards the north, determined to put as much distance between me, the city and Madame Marianne as possible.

As I walked, different voices reverberated in my head – Khadra singing of the anguish of her heart's desire, an anguish so acute it could be read on her face; the choir's *Kyrie* in the cathedral; the masked man's taunting; Madame Marianne describing our life together. All day I walked alone, passing no one, along a dusty, isolated road that climbed steadily upwards. Once or twice I thought I saw Khadra ahead of me, but it proved an illusion. As nightfall approached, I reached the crest of the final incline. Beneath me was a vast lake, surrounded by hills on all sides, the still surface of the water ominous black, beyond the reach of the rays of the disappearing sun, slipping below the ridge on which I stood. I looked back. The distance I had covered in the last two days lay mapped before me. In the gathering twilight, I could see the outline of the cathedral spire and the long, winding road along which I had travelled.

"Welcome to the Valley of the Silhouettes."

I spun around. A wizened old man was looking at me fixedly.

"Come with me. I will be your guide."

"Thank you," I replied. "Is it much further to the north?"

"No," he replied. "It lies beyond the line of hills on the far side of the valley ahead. But first you have to negotiate what lies below. I will keep you company."

Darkness was falling fast. He lit a torch from a flame emanating from a deep fissure in the rock.

The descent into the valley was steep, the path uneven. I stumbled often. Eventually, we reached a small house near the lake.

"You had better rest here until the morning."

On waking, I drew back the curtain. Day had broken, but had brought only a half-light. Through the dullness I saw that directly ahead, a short way out into the lake, was a boat-shaped island, dominated by a church with a high bell tower. I could see the bell ringing but no sound came. To the right of the church was a fortified tower and to the left, an ancient stone bridge, across which shadows were passing.

The door behind me opened.

"I hope you rested well, my friend."

"Where am I?" I asked.

"Why, you are in the Valley of the Silhouettes. Come, let me show you."

We left the house in the grey half-light.

"Does it get lighter?" I asked.

"No, it does not. The sun is never visible here in the valley."

"If that is so, why do people live here? Why not leave?"

"Some would like to, I'm sure, but others are content to stay here in obscurity, forgotten."

We walked towards the bridge, reaching on the way the ruin of an ancient temple.

"Let us sit here and observe," the old man said.

Amongst the columns, up which fingers of ivy crept, I saw people walking, but only their outline, each one a shape silhouetted against the grey, dismal background, their movements jerky, spasmodic. Those that walked together spoke animatedly but no sound came from their lips.

We got up and walked on, over the bridge and across a square towards the fortified tower, menacing in its height. Still I saw no faces, no defined features, only dark silhouettes, but after a while I began to recognise amongst them profiles of people I had known. Some seemed to recognise me, men doffing their shadowy hats and women nodding in salutation. I said good morning in reply.

"I'm afraid they cannot hear you, just as you cannot hear them. Soon, unless you continue your journey, you will become like them – a silent silhouette."

I shuddered. A familiar voice beside me spoke.

"So, Johannes, here you are, trapped, condemned to a life without substance or sound, easily forgotten. Is that not what you wanted when you ran away from the cathedral – to become a nonentity, lost in the crowd?"

"No! That is not what I wanted."

"Then why did you leave the cathedral, and not wait to see the shroud fall from your creation?"

"I lacked the courage to face judgement. Fearing I may not deserve fame is not the same as desiring obscurity. And now I want to escape from this place and complete my journey."

"Well, Johannes, it's too late. The only way you can escape is to oppose me, to put up a fight and win. And I think you lack the courage to do that too."

"Let us put it to the test."

"Ah, Johannes, what bravado! And a duel – what fun!"

"I wish to be rid of you. You have dogged my heels ever since Venice."

"Don't forget the sea monster. That was me too. I take many forms – sometimes helpful, sometimes mischievous and sometimes wicked."

"All the more reason to be rid of you."

"Let the final contest begin here in the square – a church on one side and a fortified tower on the other. Fitting, don't you think?"

A crowd of silhouettes gathered around us. Beneath a veneer of smiles and politeness we circled each other, both full of venom, our rapiers poised tip to tip ready to draw first blood. Above, crow shadows started to wheel, waiting to witness the blood we would shed. The duel began. He lunged and then I. We parried each other's weapon. No quarter was granted in our dreadful dance of death. He was fleet of foot. Twice I stumbled.

"Do you wish to continue, Johannes, or shall we adjourn until another day? Indeed, do you wish to concede?"

"No! We will continue."

The silhouettes around us were becoming increasingly animated.

The man in the smiling mask suddenly lunged, grazing my cheek.

"I nearly had you, Johannes. Come, my friend, call it a day. Surrender. The next strike might be fatal. Then where will you be? Lost in eternal limbo."

"I will not concede. I will fight to the end."

"So be it."

Once again we drew close to one another, the tips of our rapiers crossing. He began to dance a minuet to distract me. Then he closed, this time slitting my sleeve.

"Johannes, once again nearly my victim. Why don't you concede and consign yourself to silent oblivion?"

He moved away, preparing his next attack. I glimpsed Khadra's face amongst the circle of silhouettes. I heard her cry, "Johannes, don't leave me now!"

I turned just in time to parry his lunge. As he stepped back, he slipped and for a second lost his balance. I saw my chance and thrust hard beneath his chest. He fell back. Regaining his footing, once more he lunged. Yet again I parried and then thrust hard. He staggered back, slowly sinking to his knees, his rapier falling from his hand.

"I am finished. You have triumphed, Johannes. Continue your journey to seek the happiness that has eluded you."

As he spoke, the rays of the sun began to fill the twilit valley and the silhouettes gained substance and definition, became corporeal people, their voices ringing out as clearly as the church bell now did. I bent over the lifeless body and drove my rapier into his heart.

"Be gone, foul friend."

Flinging my rapier to the ground, I walked away. I was now free – of him, and to leave. Skirting the lake and then taking the pathway up into the mountains beyond, I commenced the final stage of my journey.

CHAPTER THIRTEEN

Into the Wind

Reaching the top of the pass, I turned to look back. Far below lay the lake, its water now sky blue and touched by shafts of sunlight, its stillness tranquil instead of menacing. I saw the ruins where I had sat and surveyed the silhouettes, the bridge, the island with its two towers and the square where I had slain the smiling mask. Beyond I could see the faint speck of the cathedral spire in the city of my desertion and beyond that a distant range of snow-capped mountains – perhaps the ones Khadra, Olfert and I had traversed by elephant. I had travelled far. Turning to look ahead, I sensed that my journey was nearing its end. I began my descent.

The downward gradient was not steep and I made good progress, the sun warm, the breeze cooling. But before long the horizon ahead gradually became indistinct as the weather changed. From time to time, the slowly descending cloud occasionally broke to reveal a clear view beneath an azure-blue sky. In those short moments, I thought I recognised some features of the landscape. Yet, as I approached them, each one proved an illusion, a mirage. I was not discouraged. Despite the increasingly bleak scenery and the gathering northerly wind, I still possessed an unyielding conviction that I was heading to where I wished to be, that the place I had begun my journey was not far away.

By mid-afternoon, the sun had become invisible, the sky iron grey and inhospitable, the wind sharper. I sat down beside the road, sheltering in a small cleft of rock. It was getting colder. A snowflake landed on my sleeve, then another and another. It was time to choose: to take refuge from the impending storm or to walk on. I saw ahead of me a multitude of dark, sombre trees, their tops already bending in the whistling wind. Though leafless, they would surely provide some cover. I got to my feet. Behind me, the way I had come had disappeared from sight, while the way ahead was veiled by falling snow. As I walked, I thought I heard a child's voice in the distance. I stopped to listen but could hear only the bitter wind, now howling through the trees. I pressed on, but walking became more difficult as the snow deepened. I stumbled several times but still I went on. It was becoming ever colder and my jacket offered scant protection. I recalled the cautionary words of the wagoner. After a while the trees became fewer and though the wind howled less it felt sharper as it cut into my face, its vicious chill even more intense. There was no longer a horizon, nor any visible feature in the snow-hidden landscape, just an accursed obliteration of white. All I knew was that with the northerly wind ahead of me, I was still heading towards my destination.

Two gnarled trees, close together, suddenly appeared like ghosts in the gloom. I stood in the lee of the larger of the two to gather my thoughts. I was chilled to the core. My hands were blue despite being thrust in my pockets. I knew that if I remained still for much longer my remaining spirits would ebb away to become as frozen as the ground on which I stood. Once more, I heard above the noise of the cruel and unremitting wind a voice – a child's. Perhaps there was a child ahead of me lost in the snow. Again I heard it, fainter this time. If it was indeed a lost child, I knew I had to search for it while I still had some strength. I moved from the shelter of the tree and stumbled on into the deep drifts of snow. The wind once more gathered strength, blowing harder than before. I was rigid and aching with cold but still I was driven on by an inner force, urging me not to surrender, not to lie down and sleep. I cannot say how much longer I fought the pain of each step, but as night descended my diminishing spirits became even more tested. Then I fell. Try as I might, I could not regain my feet, leaving me confined to crawling. I looked ahead. Nothing but blackness and the whistling wind. It was surely time to succumb to the lure of sleep. My hands and knees gave way.

"Johannes, is this how you wish to be remembered – as the artist who perished in a snowstorm, the artist who gave up, who became nature's victim? That is not the Johannes I once knew. He would have pressed on, driven by his stubbornness, refused to give up."

I struggled to raise myself from the tomb of snow the wind was building around me, to see who was uttering these words, but I could make out only the form of a hooded figure.

"Here, take my hand."

It was warm and soft. Holding it tight, I staggered to my feet, peering through the driving snow to try to see the face inside the hood.

"It is me, Marianne. I am sure you remember me, from the Black Wolf tavern. I am the one they sometimes call the sorceress."

Her profile was just as I had drawn her, but her face was younger, beautiful, almost illuminated. Her cloak bore no flakes of snow.

"Johannes, take courage. Walk on. You do not have much further to travel. Two nights ago, when we were together, I punished you with thorns for what you once did to me – for spurning me, preferring the pursuit of your art, and driving me into the arms of another in a country for which I had no affinity. Your body bears the marks of my vengeance. Soon, the scars will vanish. Have faith. Take this. It will protect you and be a reminder of me."

She placed in my hand the small carving she had held in her fingers when we lay together. It felt warm. I looked up but she had vanished. I turned once more into the driving snow and the bitter, remorseless wind, the carving clasped tightly in my hand. Again, I cannot say how much longer I laboured in the darkness, but this time my spirits seemed to lift with each step I took. Gradually, the wind eased, the snow ceased and stars began to appear in the sky. Soon, I entered a forest, the branches of the trees seeming to dip in salutation. Through the shifting configuration of time-thickened trunks I saw a cloaked figure playing a lute. I ran forward but when I reached the spot the figure was nowhere to be seen, just the lingering sound of the melody whispering in the leaves. I walked on, sure that my journey was at an end, that I had reached the north.

CHAPTER FOURTEEN

Confusion of Harmonies

Weary but with a lighter heart, I continued, more and more certain that I was close to my destination, to where I had started my journey. Leaving the forest and the sweet melody behind me, I soon entered into darkness, that unsettling interval of silence and inky blackness before dawn when the presiding terrors of the night mount a final siege before beginning their surrender to approaching daylight. Unable to see, I paused for a minute or so, despite the bitter cold, in an effort to regain my bearings.

Suddenly, a narrow streak of blood-red light appeared on the distant horizon, steadily widening into a broadening band of brightness, much as I had seen before on the boat as we approached landfall in the east. As the brightness began to intensify from red to yellow, I saw that I stood on a vast open plain, whose only noticeable features were scatterings of scarred, leafless trees, the bent-over relics of some bygone destructive wind. Billowing clouds quickly formed in the sky, constantly shaping and reshaping, displaying a kaleidoscope of vivid colours, as though reflecting a great fire raging unseen in the distance. About me, exotic animals and a prodigality of peacocks strutted with exultant pride. Rats scuttled into the cracked earth, while fantastic birds took flight. Loud, discordant, pulsating music replaced the earlier tuneful melody of the forest. The ground on which I stood seemed to tremble with every beat. I stood, rooted, amazed by the confusion unfolding before me, struggling to comprehend the meaning of such visual and auditory disharmony.

"Welcome to the north," a stentorian voice called out.

I spun around to see who had extended the greeting but no one was there.

As the music, bar by bar, began to become less dissonant, more pleasing to the ear, the ground shook once more and from widening fissures small human figures emerged. They formed a circle, slowly moving around me. At first their features were indistinct, but as they grew in height and the light from the sky increased – still reflecting red, yellow and blue as from the ferocious flames of a distant fire – their faces became clearer. It seemed to me that all the people I had ever met, all those with whom I had crossed paths, whether in friendship, indifference or hostility, were engaged in a courtly dance, revolving in an ever-deepening circle with me at its centre. Some smiled, some scowled and some even pointed an accusatory finger at me. As the circle turned and each figure passed me, they nodded, seemingly confirming to some unseen presence their acquaintance with me; though their lips moved, I could hear no words. The music was now that of flutes, pleasantly tuneful and light of touch. With each change of tempo and volume, the circle, moving alternately clockwise and anti-clockwise, responded, quickening and slowing its steps, swelling and diminishing as more dancers joined or departed.

Then, with a sudden burst of trumpets and violins, the circle began to disappear, replaced by tableaux from my life – scenes of both action and reflection performed by actors, some of whose faces I could recognise and some not. As the music slowly reduced in volume, I tried to hear the words of those in each tableau but to no avail. The actors remained mute, offering only the enigma of silent charades.

Three elaborately dressed figures emerged from one scene, as though stepping from a Venetian carnival, inviting me to dance with them re-enactments of some of the deeds I had committed. Dragged onto their stage, I was obliged to join them. To the accompaniment of an even louder blast of trumpets, horns and shrill violins and the hissing of giant flames on the horizon, I became part of a new circle, performing a stately gavotte followed by a courtly sarabande, reliving with each partner a few fleeting moments of a particular episode of my life in which they had featured, participating in pleasurable memories and uncomfortable truths. With each elaborate step of this *danse macabre*, I came face to face with a fragment of my past – friends, foes, clients desirable and undesirable, those I had loved and those I despised. As I exchanged one partner for another, each whispered – smiling all the time – a truth or untruth in my ear.

With the music dying once more, the circle fell away and gradually vanished, leaving me alone on the empty plain. Still the mighty fire on the horizon burned but the clouds slowly began to disappear, as though some unseen hand were drawing back massive curtains, to reveal the boundless universe, similar to the spectacle I had seen in La Serenissima. For a brief moment, enormous indistinct gaseous figures appeared to float across the firmament, discharging atoms of light and an intense, almost ear-splitting sound. Everything around me seemed to burn. I struggled to breathe. My clothes became unbearable to my skin. And higher and higher into the sky rose a great orb, unbearable to the eye.

Shielding my gaze, I looked down and, to the sound of a host of shrill whistles, saw the ground around me slowly become green and a stream form. Once more I could draw breath in comfort. The previous discord, the confusion of disharmonies, had vanished, replaced by a recognisable order in which the natural elements, once described by the Ancient Greeks, were once more in balance. In place of frightening instability was reassuring stability, accompanied by the gentle sound of far-off flutes and other pleasing instruments. I looked back. The previous darkness had disappeared. Birds had begun to sing; the trees had straightened and regained their height and verdure. I looked up at the sky, now deep blue, cloudless and with the sun in its rightful position. Gone was the distant raging fire. The air was crisp and chilling but refreshing. I started walking once again and with each step the landscape became more heartening, more comforting. Though fatigued and cold, I knew I would soon be where I had begun.

Finally, I entered the great edifice to which Khadra's lute had led me an incalculable time ago, my head ringing with the sound of a rousing fanfare of triumph from a silent organ. I sat to contemplate not just the awe-inducing testament to God and craftsmanship around me but to reflect on my journey, the moments of joy and pleasure and those of fear, sadness and pain. I recalled Khadra, my companion on that journey, who like me had been searching for a destination, a truth. Now I had reached my journey's end but she had not reached hers. For as long as hers remained unfulfilled, we were, wherever she was, still bound by an adamantine bond – the pursuit of an elusive, still unresolved truth. But there was no longer anything I could do. After many vicissitudes I had returned to the north. I could go no further. Khadra and I were each alone, on separate paths. Exhausted, I fell asleep.

"You should not be here. You must leave."

The voice was half familiar. I struggled to open my eyes. I was so cold, my hands and feet were numb. I closed my eyes once more, unable to stay awake.

"I urge you to stir," the voice persisted. "You cannot stay here. We must go home – now! You cannot be seen here. Quickly, come with me."

"But why should I leave? I have reached the north. My journey is complete. I cannot go further."

"You must come now!"

I struggled to my feet.

"So be it," I replied.

PART TWO

Edda's Story

CHAPTER FIFTEEN

Secrets and Silence

The bricks and mortar of ancient houses rarely divulge to passers-by what they have heard or witnessed. It is more often left to the curious to draw back the secretive curtain to discover, or more likely those with loose tongues to reveal, the happenings – whether death, madness, jealousy, betrayal, rage or joy – that may have left an indelible but silent imprint on the fabric of the building and the lives of the family within.

I, Edda, long the milkmaid in this house and regarded by some as a gossip as I go about my daily work, have chosen to share with you the story of this house on Herengracht and of its occupants, the family of Johannes Peeters. For too long, nothing has been said. I, for one, have held my tongue, refrained from the gossip I am accused of. People walk past, cast a glance at the shuttered windows and walk on, wondering for a moment or two, perhaps, what really happened here all those years ago, not only after the event in the cathedral but before it, and why to this day the house appears silent, lifeless, forlorn. Then there are the eavesdroppers, those who find an excuse to linger by the often open window of the *voorhuis* – perhaps when exchanging the time of day or stopping on the pretext of peddling some item of clothing, kitchenware or food – in the hope of overhearing some snippet of conversation amongst the servants and gaining an insight into life in the inner reaches of this house.

But I have decided that you, an interested, concerned passer-by who has occasionally, as I have noticed, lingered longer than most when walking past, should hear more than others about what happened. Besides, soon it will be my last day in employment here. Though somewhat advanced in age, my lover of many years has proposed and I have accepted, but when we shall actually be married remains to be seen. So, with my chores for today largely done, I have decided to invite you into the *voorhuis* to hear my story of number 7 Herengracht. Please come in. And wipe your shoes on the mat.

Where shall I begin? At the cathedral, or before that day, when the master married the young and beautiful Marianne? I have observed you, from the window, to be an infrequent visitor to these parts and therefore no doubt not entirely familiar with our city, so I am sure you will want to hear about the well-known altarpiece, about what happened on the day it was unveiled. But I think it is best if I begin with her, Marianne – or Annemieke, as the master called her in an effort to disguise her French parentage. As you might imagine, the French were not liked around here at the time, given the profoundly warlike disposition of King Louis of France towards our country.

It is unclear how they met. Master Johannes' father, Jan, was a wealthy entrepreneur, a successful trader – indeed he owned two large ships that plied the coasts even down to Italy. He hoped, like other fathers do, that his son would eventually follow in his footsteps and continue to expand the family business. But Jan had other ambitions too. Even when older, he still held on to the notion that he might one day be chosen to become mayor of the city. But by all accounts, notably from what the other servants told me when I first came to this house, he was not a popular man – too preoccupied with wealth and flaunting it, as some claimed. Thus he never received encouragement to join the council, where many feared he might have excessive influence, and heaven forbid that he should ever become mayor. Whether that bothered him is hard to say. Perhaps not. Instead, his business grew, giving him the financial means to extend this house and acquire a bigger storehouse for his goods.

Master Johannes grew up quickly and, before he was twenty, set sail – at his father's insistence, but with evident reluctance – on one of the company's ships to learn how to buy and sell. He was absent for several months, returned and almost immediately left again, but this time he seemed most keen to go. The elderly seamstress, Wilhelmina, told us she thought the twinkle in his eye meant he had met a girl.

"I know that boy. He's in love. Whether his father will approve is another matter. He has a match in mind for Master Johannes, though his late wife – God rest her soul – would not have liked his choice, that's for sure."

Master Johannes had not long been back from his second voyage when his father fell ill and took to his bed. Though it was clear he was eager to sail again, the master accepted his father's wish that he should remain in the city.

It was during this time that we servants began to see a change in him. It appeared to us he was losing interest in his father's business, and whenever he was not helping his ailing father with the accounts or other matters of trade, he would be painting. Sometimes, when Master Johannes was out, we used to creep into his room to glance at the drawings and canvases he kept in a large cupboard. Many were of the same young woman. Wilhelmina said his apparent obsession with every detail of her clothes – judging by the intricate presentation of the ribbons in her hair and the French fashion of her dresses, some of which were quite revealing at the bust and ankles – surely meant she was the girl with whom he had fallen in love. After all, he had rarely been seen with a local girl in the city.

Before long, his father showed signs of improvement and, as the coastal trade was encountering some hard times, he readily consented to Johannes undertaking another voyage to sell as much merchandise as possible. Thus Master Johannes set sail once more. Oh, he was so happy that day! He even came into the kitchen and gave us each a kiss.

While the master was at sea, his father suffered a relapse and became grievously ill. The doctors confined him to bed in the hope that would help to conserve his diminishing strength until the master came home. He survived until his son's return, but died a few days afterwards. The following weeks were ones of desolation but the master assured us that, though he intended eventually to sell the business in order to become an artist, he would ensure there was sufficient income for us to remain in Herengracht. During this time there was frequent correspondence between the master and a woman in France, Madame Franmery. From the number of letters we were asked to dispatch and the delight he showed when her letters arrived, it became clear to us that it was his intention they should marry and that she, as his wife, should become the chatelaine of the house. And so it proved. Within some six months of his father's death, the master left once more by boat, not so much to buy and sell staple commodities but, we all agreed, to import a luxury – a wife. The prospect filled us with trepidation.

Before I tell you about her, perhaps, as the others are out, I should let you have a glimpse of the house beyond the *voorhuis*, to see how grand it is. You'll have noticed on your walks along the Herengracht that unlike many of our neighbours' houses this one has a wider front, indicating a property of some distinction and an owner of considerable wealth.

As I'm sure you know, the *voorhuis*, where we are standing now, is the point of contact between us inside and the street outside. Beyond that open window is the city, while beyond this door is the master's world. That of the mistress of the house is beyond his, at the back, and leads to a pleasant yard with a tree and benches. Unless the weather is bad or too cold, we usually have the *voorhuis* window open so we can chat with those we like the look of – indeed, that is how I met the man I will shortly, God willing, marry – and, of course, pick up city gossip that we might otherwise miss, even on our trips to the open-air markets, where all too often there is little time to chinwag with those plying their trade. And with the window open, we can hear the church bells and tuneful carillons – important for knowing not just the hour of the day but how much time we have left to complete our daily chores.

Now, if you promise to be quiet and follow me, I will let you take a peek into the inner world of this house – the world that a passer-by like you never sees. If the master knew what I was doing I would get into so much trouble.

As you see, these rooms are formally aligned – *en enfilade* is the term. And dark – gloomy, even. The floor is tiled – easier to keep clean than carpets, I don't mind telling you – some white tiles but the majority smaller and reddish in colour. Nothing special. You'll find them in most of the houses around here. The same goes for those windows there on the right: a row of three, high, narrow, leaded – typical of the local architecture. Not that you can see them behind the curtains. The richness of that deep red and the thickness of the material – they're the best money can buy. We keep them drawn nowadays, though they make the room even darker. All the furniture is of high quality, expensive, solid. I say "all" but as you see it's minimal. A fair amount's been sold in recent years. The large fireplace opposite the windows is in use all year round. Even in summer the house can be chill and damp.

Before we go through to the next room I should point out the portrait on the wall to the right of the door – though you could hardly miss a picture that big. That's the master's father, painted shortly before he became ill. It's a good likeness. He was already elderly by then, but still a powerful presence. He always wore his beard in that style, and always dressed in black from head to toe but with some conspicuous token of his wealth and standing. The distinguished-looking badge around his neck was awarded to him in Venice. And on the table beneath the portrait is a model of the ship on which the master sailed, the one on which he brought back his wife.

Now, if you'd like to follow me into the next room … There's not much I need to tell you about this one, or the one beyond. As you can see, there are large windows on the right and smaller, higher ones on the left, all with the curtains drawn, as is our habit. Most of the paintings on the wall were painted by Master Johannes.

Which brings us to this room at the back. I shouldn't really be showing it to you, as it was occupied by the mistress of the house. We keep it locked now. But in many ways it's the heart of the house's story. Come in. Some find it cold, lifeless. They don't like the dark landscapes on the walls – the undulating hills and forests obviously not this land. The harpsichord in the corner is as elegant as the mistress was. She played beautifully. And the high-backed red upholstered chair was her favourite. That door in the other corner leads to a small yard. The mistress was fond of this room. She regarded it as her personal realm and accordingly forbade her husband to enter. Many things happened here – initially happy but, later, things with unhappy consequences for us all.

I think it's time for us to retrace our steps back to the *voorhuis*. The staircase, half hidden in the gloom? That leads upstairs. Obviously I cannot take you there. That's where the master is.

You say you're struck by the darkness, the silence and the pervasive sadness of what you have seen. You are right. I'm so used to it I hardly notice any more.

But still, it's here, in the *voorhuis*, that I feel most at ease. My master painted me in this room once, just as I am today. My clothes, simple and coarse. Plain – scraped-back hair and this white cap are hardly flattering – and workmanlike with my sleeves rolled back and my overskirt hitched up. He even included the table at which we are sitting, complete with pitchers of milk, and baskets of bread and apples. There was dignity and beauty in the scene, he said. Lord knows where he found it. I've been happy here, yet I can't help but smile when I think I'll be leaving soon and starting a new episode in my life. Talking of pitchers, can I offer you some milk? Yes? There you are.

Now, where was I? Ah yes, madame. I will never forget the day of her arrival.

She was truly beautiful, with a captivating smile, and richly dressed in a fine à la mode gown, no doubt all the rage in France, where they had married. The master was so proud of her, so attentive to her. In the ensuing weeks, he must have spent a fortune, buying her new furniture, more elegant clothes imported from France and purchasing the harpsichord you have just seen. Each morning she would sit for over an hour at her dressing table, attending to her hair and complexion with the help of her French maid, Sybille. She spoke little to us, relying on Sybille to convey her wishes.

For many months it was a bright and happy house. Then a gradual but noticeable change took place. The master became distracted and the mistress, ever beautiful and beguiling, increasingly capricious, arrogant and dismissive. There were times when we overheard her speaking cruelly to the master. Trying to satisfy her increasingly unreasonable demands but frequently offended by the similarly increasing ungraciousness of her manner, the master's mood became darker. He lost all semblance of interest in his father's business, the recording of accounts fell behind and he spent more time painting in his studio upstairs, locking the door so she could not enter. That enraged her. We couldn't avoid hearing the rancorous arguments between them and the even stronger fits of temper on her part, often complaining about being bereft of her friends and the social entertainment she had enjoyed in France – a country she bitterly regretted leaving.

They went away to France for several weeks. Upon their return, they appeared in better spirits, physically closer to one another, as though a boil had been lanced. One day not too long afterwards, the master came to see us in a state of great happiness to announce that the mistress was with child. He became even more attentive to her, anxious to satisfy her every whim. Her confinement was not easy and we did our best to help her through some difficult months. For his part, the master spent as much time as he could trying to revive his declining business, but the constant conflict with France did not make this straightforward. To his delight and the mistress's relief, she gave birth to a girl – beautiful, like her mother. They called her Marie Angélique. Immediately, we secured a wet nurse. In the weeks and months that followed, the mistress paid less and less attention to the child, with the result that for much of the day Marie Angélique was with us in the *voorhuis*. Sometimes, we used to let her peer through the keyhole of her father's studio. As she received few gifts from her mother and father, one day I gave her a locket containing an image of the Virgin and Child, which she wore proudly around her neck, refusing ever to remove it.

As trade became more difficult, the master's business began to incur heavy debts and eventually he was obliged to sell quickly both the business and the two vessels. We were told they fetched a reasonable sum, but after payment of his debts and still more expenditure for the mistress, he was left with only a small, modest income. He decided that rather than use this money to finance a new, smaller trading business, he would make a few investment deposits to earn some interest for the mistress's expenses and the maintenance of the house and household, and try to make a living as an artist. He had already painted several portraits of friends and acquaintances, the quality of which had led to regular commissions, providing some additional income. But while those who sought paintings by him were generous with their praise, they often drove a hard bargain when it came to price. Nonetheless, he persevered and slowly but steadily the prestige and frequency of the commissions improved. Increasingly, he spent more time in his studio and before long the mistress began to accuse him – quite unfairly, in our opinion – of desertion. Yet despite the vicissitudes of their life together, the marriage survived, at times even seeming to flourish. And whatever the problems in his business and marriage, the master doted on the child.

Then came tragedy. One day, when Marie Angélique was aged three, she disappeared from the yard at the back of the house. In the days and weeks of constant searching that followed, the master was distraught, as indeed was the mistress, though she seemed to bear their daughter's disappearance with greater calm and resignation. Despite strenuous efforts the child was never found. There was much gossip, innuendo and finger-pointing about her fate, many believing she had fallen into the canal, some saying that she had been abducted and even taken away by boat. It was a terrible blow, from which to this day the master and this house have never recovered. On that day, it was as though a dark, menacing shadow had fallen over the house.

Any hope of finding the child gradually evaporated. During the next year or so, life resumed a regular if cheerless pattern. On advice, the master invested some of the increased income from the sale of his paintings in other commercial and financial activities. But even this was not enough for him to afford the luxuries to which the mistress had long been accustomed. Twice she went away to visit her family in France and on each occasion, after an absence of many weeks, she returned with a new wardrobe of clothes. Where the money came from was not clear. On the second occasion, she returned with a young boy, her nephew, she claimed, who would be staying for some time. The master warmly welcomed the boy and soon they became close friends. This friendship helped to distract him from the unpredictable behaviour of the mistress but his greatest solace remained painting – not just portrait commissions but also street scenes for his own pleasure, so he said. As his skill in portrait painting became better known, more clients, both new and existing, came to him with commissions for family portraits to hang on their walls to record their climb up the social ladder. He received many compliments on his work, but gradually became tired of the jobbing nature of this kind of art, which seemed increasingly to disillusion him. He told us one day, after a particularly obnoxious client had left, that he sought a greater challenge. Shortly afterwards, he decided to enter a guild competition to paint a new altarpiece for the cathedral. Much to our surprise, his proposal was accepted and he won the commission. Its award turned life in this house on its head, bringing great sadness and leading many to think that the master had become afflicted by demons, that he had lost his mind.

But I'm forgetting my manners. Let me pour you some more milk.

And now we have company.

Saskia, you're back earlier than I expected. I can see from your full bag that you have had a successful trip to the market, and from the gleam in your eye that you have news to share. But it will have to wait. We have a guest. This gentleman was passing by, as he does from time to time. I have always liked his smile and the cheery way he doffs his cap – to me, the milkmaid, of all people! I was just telling him about the day the master left. Sir, this is Saskia, our cook, as you probably guessed from her long white apron, her heat-reddened face – and her girth! Now now, Saskia, you know I mean nothing by it. Sit down with us. You were present that morning, and remember the day of rage as vividly as I do. You can tell me if I miss anything.

So, to continue.

The master came down early from his room that morning. I remember every detail. He wore his painting clothes, as he called them – a slashed black jacket over a white shirt, black britches, red stockings and of course his black cap. I will never forget his words.

"To complete the commission in peace and good order, I have decided to establish my studio for this work in the cathedral sacristy. There I will be each day, returning home in the evening or perhaps sleeping there overnight. The boy can be my assistant, helping me with the preparation and bringing me food. Do not fret about my decision. The altarpiece is a titanic challenge, which I am determined to complete. This is the only way I can do so. Your mistress will be in charge of this house in my absence."

With that he left and we didn't see him again for more than two years, our master confining himself to that cold, forbidding, desolate place, never setting foot outside. To everyone, even to us, who loved him, he became a lost soul, but the councillor, Hendricks, insisted he had faith in him. Others on the council, however, did not, commissioning in due course – and against Hendricks' advice – another artist to begin a different altarpiece. What treachery was that! The mistress was at first stricken by the master's decision but she soon adjusted to his absence, excising him from her life. She forbade us to visit him. Soon, he became forgotten, some in the marketplace putting it about that he had lost his sanity and, for the sake of the family name, had been locked away, some even saying that he was dead.

For those two years, the mistress reigned supreme at the house. The merchants and financiers with whom the master had invested money, from the sale both of his father's business and of his paintings, became frequent visitors. She often entertained the wealthy of the city to evenings of music, card playing and good food. She wore fine clothes, remained striking and was much flattered. Soon she had acquired a lover and another after him …

Please pardon my hesitation. It's not easy to confess the sins of one's mistress, to reveal secrets long hidden within the walls of this house. But it is important for the truth to be known. Saskia is squeezing my hand. She agrees with me. Well, then.

One morning, I received an instruction to take some milk to my mistress's room. I went up. She was still completing her toilet, attended by Sybille, who was lacing the bodice of her shift. I stood and watched, transfixed, as she stepped into an elegant, shimmering gown of white satin I had not seen her wear before. I remember that dress to this day – its glinting highlights, the dark shadows of the folds of the skirt and the overall scattering of soft reflected light from the open window. I could not help but be aware of the contrast with my own coarse, sombre clothing. Taking a last look in the mirror of vanity, she turned to me.

"Edda, you know what you have to do. Sybille cannot do everything!"

Putting the milk to one side, I picked up the large shallow silver bowl and held it as the mistress gently washed her hands in the water Sybille poured from a silver pitcher. I had long been taught that this cleansing gesture was a rich woman's symbolic demonstration of her purity, but the words I was about to hear her deliver made it instead a cynical denial of fidelity. I recalled the plays I had seen performed in the cathedral at Easter, in which Pilot washed his hands of responsibility for our Lord on the day of His crucifixion. Then the mistress spoke directly to me.

"Edda, I believe your master is lost to madness. By locking himself away from all contact, he has forsworn his every obligation to me. I have concluded that he no longer loves me. He does not share my bed, thereby denying my existence as his wife. I loved him once, but no longer. Accordingly, as you have just witnessed, I wash my hands of all commitment to him, all responsibility for him. I regard my marriage to him to be at an end. I have met a new love and together he and I will begin a fresh future. I bear his child. We will be leaving shortly. In my absence, this house and all that is in it, including you and the other servants, will continue to belong to me and you will follow my instructions as and when you receive them. To be clear, the man who was once master here is no longer welcome in this house. Is that understood?"

I nodded.

"You may go now. Please have the carriage brought around quickly."

This news, which I immediately relayed to Saskia, Wilhelmina and the others, caused us great consternation and sadness but it also stoked an inner rage at such vile treatment of the master, who was and would continue to be unaware of her treachery. Over the ensuing weeks, the mistress and her lover, whose name we could not bear to utter, came and went, his behaviour equally flagrant and upsetting. Soon, as her belly swelled, they prepared for a longer journey, with no indication of when they might return. It gave us great relief when they, and Sybille, departed. But her nephew, a sweet boy, was commanded to accompany them too. We were sad to see him go and it was evident he was reluctant to do so. We drew the curtains, covered the furniture with drapes. When Wilhelmina encountered a gypsy in the marketplace, she asked her to curse the mistress. In the church, we prayed for our master, urging the Lord to restore his sanity.

A year later the mistress returned, without her lover and without a child, said by Sybille to have died in early infancy from a fever. And also without her nephew. She lived alone in her downstairs room, reading or playing doleful tunes on the harpsichord and refusing to see all visitors. Only Sybille was allowed to approach her. Within six months she died, from a broken heart and an overdose of laudanum according to the physician. She was buried without ceremony, with us as her only mourners. Lawyers informed us that she had left no will, so that for the present the small income from the remaining investments would be used to maintain the house and staff until the master's future had been resolved. Once more, the house was enveloped in a cloak of tragedy and uncertainty. Wilhelmina and the others could take no more and, with Sybille's departure, only Saskia and I were left. We stayed out of loyalty to the master but, in our hearts, we believed that the house was slowly dying and us with it.

Was that the end of the story, you ask, having seen the dark, silent rooms I showed you earlier? No. It was not.

One morning came the unexpected news that the altarpiece had been completed and that within days it would be taken from the sacristy to be hung above the high altar. There was much curiosity as to what it would depict and even greater speculation about the fate of our master. Would he emerge insane? What did he know of his wife's behaviour and demise? As for Councillor Hendricks, now the mayor, he came under great pressure to hang the alternative altarpiece the council had commissioned, but he stood firm and persuaded the bishop that all would be well.

The great day arrived. The doors of the cathedral were flung open. The city fathers and their families arrived in good time to take their seats. The panels of the rood screen had been removed so that the congregation had a clear view the length of the nave. With the assistance of the mayor, Saskia and I managed to secure a place in a packed side chapel adjacent to the high altar. A huge dark-red shroud hung in place of the old altarpiece, which had been damaged some years previously by marauding French soldiers. The Mass began. We looked around anxiously, as did the mayor, to try to catch sight of the master, but he was nowhere to be seen. Then came the moment of unveiling. As the choir sang the *Sanctus* in a great reverberating voice, the priests either side of the altar tugged the four long white cords and the shroud, after an initial hesitation, began to slip, falling slowly away as shafts of sunlight suddenly penetrated the nave through the high windows.

A loud gasp swept through the cathedral. The bishop, priests and acolytes fell to their knees in astonishment, the serried ranks of the congregation following likewise. The medieval style of the previous altarpiece had gone. In its place was a remarkable, truly lifelike image, the simple frame of the portrait and its two side panels adding to its natural impact. The Virgin's richly textured gown, the silky fineness of her cascading hair, the landscape behind her with elephants and camels, the complexity of shadow and light – further enhanced by the sunlight flooding the high altar – and the shadow her gown cast on the background in the painting gave her even greater presence. She bore no crown, no heavenly adornment. Instead, her gentle smile, the pride of motherhood evident on her face as she held the Christ Child, her right hand extended as though greeting the congregation, transfixed not only Saskia and me but everyone. For minutes, the church was silent until the choir, led by the mighty organ, sang "*O quam gloriosum*".

The Mass ended. Many people surged forward to view the painting closer to, words of praise and admiration for the artist pouring from their mouths. Others left, some troubled by a depiction of the Virgin so different from the style they were used to. For the rest of the day, people came in large numbers to see what fast became the talk of the city. There were expressions of great pride and approval, but also criticism and charges of blasphemy since it presented the realistic likeness of a woman and not an idealised impression of the Virgin. Such was the strength of the reaction, both for and against, that the mayor provided a guard at the cathedral for several days. But soon the mood eased and before long there was widespread acclaim for the new altarpiece – much, I might add, to the pleasure of the mayor, whose term of office the city extended, in gratitude. The alternative altarpiece was locked away, ignored. Nothing was left of the master's *modello* or his other materials, equipment and belongings. He had destroyed everything.

One evening a day or so after the unveiling, Saskia and I returned to the cathedral as the great doors were being shut and bolted for the night. We begged the verger to allow us in, so that we could get near to the altarpiece. After some hesitation, he agreed. Almost alone in the cathedral, we stood in awe before the painting, which was even more wondrous in the candlelight. Then Saskia suddenly exclaimed and pointed.

"Look, Edda, look!"

In the bottom left-hand corner of the painting was a young child playing a lute, a tender, faithful representation of Marie Angélique – she was even wearing the locket I had given her around her neck. The master had captured her, singing to the Virgin. It was profoundly moving, to see that he had remembered her in his painting. Do you recall, Saskia, you fell to your knees in tears, quite overcome? And that the verger then drew our attention to the scarcely visible words, *Arte nulli secundus*, in the other corner of the painting, inscribed on one of the pillars depicted in the middle distance? He explained that it meant *By art, second to none.*

That night we went home filled with joy at what we had witnessed, though our happiness was somewhat diminished by the failure of the master to return. We had not seen him in the cathedral, neither had the mayor. A monk had reported that a bearded, dishevelled man hurriedly left the adjacent abbey in great distress at the time of the dedication Mass, and another report said he had been seen leaving the city. A few weeks later the master was found living some distance away, alone. A priest established his true identity and, once he had done so, persuaded him to return home. He was in poor condition – emaciated, disoriented and much aged.

We have done our utmost to care for him in the years since then. His strength has improved, but he remains reclusive, unable, with his faltering memory, to remember many things. We explained the death of his wife but he never speaks of her. Some evenings he goes to the cathedral and sits looking at the altarpiece, quietly talking to himself, his troubled, confused and obsessed mind trying to imagine where his beloved daughter might be, what has become of her. He tells us stories of what he believes she is doing. Usually, Saskia or I will have to go to the cathedral to bring him home. As we walk back to Herengracht, he keeps repeating, "I knew her. She was my companion. I let her down." At night, he often wakes from what are clearly, for him, the horrors of the small, silent hours – distressing dreams, nightmares and other deliriums that constantly beset him in what he sometimes describes, in his calmer moments, as a battle between surrender and implacable conscience. It is heartbreaking to see him suffer such affliction – self-inflicted wounds of the mind. We comfort him as best we can.

Today, just like every other day, he rests in his room, staring out of the window, saying little, oblivious to the praise he continues to receive for the altarpiece so many admire. We go about our business, looking after him and this house. But as you have observed, it remains a house of sadness, shadows and silence. It's like a single candle burning in impenetrable darkness. One day it will be extinguished and everything that has happened will be forgotten, unremembered.

There, dear passer-by, I have told you the full story of this unhappy house. There's no more to be said.

You ask again about the master's child. Nothing further was

heard of her, no trace ever found. Whether she fell into the canal, was abducted, or even given away by her mother, as some have claimed, has never been established. She simply vanished. All that is left of her is her image on the altarpiece, a small child playing a lute. The instrument she is holding resembles the one she was once given by a stranger who came to this house one day to enquire about the possibility of the master painting his portrait. He said that he had purchased it in the marketplace to take home to his granddaughter but, having seen Marie Angélique and been moved by her playing of the child-size lute, he thought that he would give it to her for when she was older rather than carry it home. The child loved that lute and, like the locket around her neck, would never let it go. She had it with her in the yard on the day she disappeared. It too was never found.

So, passer-by, that is all there is to say. The end of a sad story indeed.

CHAPTER SIXTEEN

Khadra

I see the house has drawn you back. I'm glad I caught sight of you, walking past the open window, as I was sitting here with little to do other than watch the world go by, waiting for my husband-to-be. I apologise for my rudeness in calling out. You smiled and doffed your cap as usual, before continuing on your way along the canal. I had to call again to make you stop. But tomorrow I will be gone, to be married and live elsewhere, and since we talked … the end of the story … there is a twist to it. Would you like me to share it with you? Now that you have turned back, won't you come in and have a drink of milk, as before? Good, now sit back and listen to what I have to say.

Not long after you passed this way the last time, the city became agog at the news that the celebrated musician and composer, Cecilia de la Roche, would be visiting the city en route to play at the court of King Augustus the Strong. What's more, she had agreed that during her short stay she would perform two of her compositions in the cathedral, and thus see the altarpiece, which she had heard about because of its spreading fame and the continuing debate about its style.

Cecilia de la Roche was said to be famous not only for her music and her beauty but also for carrying a lute wherever she went – though, we were told, she rarely played it as the instrument was now no longer popular. As a result, there was naturally much interest in her intended performance. It was arranged that she and her small retinue would stay for several days in a large house, near to the mayor's, further along the Herengracht.

I was sitting in the *voorhuis* – the window open, as usual – when I saw her carriage go past. It was grand, black in colour with an impressive coat of arms on the door. As you can imagine, there was much hustle and bustle in the street. Later that day, I received a message from the kitchen of the house where she was staying, asking if I would go early the next morning with extra milk and help prepare breakfast for some twenty people. I was nervous at the prospect but equally excited at the possibility of seeing such an acclaimed musician and composer – a woman, and a beautiful one, at that. For me, a simple milkmaid, it would be a huge honour. I realised the chances were small, though, as I would just be in the kitchen.

I got up extra early the next day – the day of her concert – and after helping to prepare the master I arrived at the house along the canal. There was great excitement and hurrying and scurrying. I poured the milk and did all that I was asked to do. I was about to leave, having no further tasks to complete, when I received an urgent instruction to take some more milk to the rooms upstairs. Guided by a chambermaid, I did so, leaving small jugs outside the rooms as she directed. Then, just as I was about to make my way back downstairs, a door opened and she appeared – the lady herself, the musician. I could not believe my eyes. She was wearing a low-cut gown and around her slender neck hung a small locket, just like the one with an image of the Virgin and Child inside that I had given Marie Angélique. I suddenly felt faint. She took my arm.

"What on earth is the matter? You look as though you have seen a ghost – you're as white as the milk in the pitcher you've just put down. Are you unwell?"

I burst into uncontrollable tears.

"Come into my room. Tell me what's wrong."

I tried hard to compose myself.

"Madame, excuse me. I am so sorry to have disturbed you. Please forgive me. I will leave immediately."

"Have I done something to offend you?"

"No, madame not all." Once more, I could not contain my tears.

"Please sit and tell me what's the matter."

I summoned the courage.

"Madame, I am a milkmaid in a large house further along the Herengracht. Many years ago, the mistress of the house had a child, whom they called Marie Angélique. She was such a beautiful little girl. She spent a lot of time with us in the kitchen – it was her favourite place to be. Because I adored her, not having had children of my own, one day I gave her a locket, just like the one you are wearing – a plain, simple locket, with an image of the Virgin and Child inside – to keep. She loved it, placing it immediately around her neck, and refused ever to take it off. Then at the age of three she disappeared – simply vanished from the yard. No one ever knew what had happened to her. We were all distraught. Her father – my master – became an artist and some years ago he painted a fine altarpiece which now hangs in the cathedral where I believe you are to perform. In one corner of it is a picture of a child – his daughter, Marie Angélique – playing a lute and wearing my locket around her neck. Seeing a similar one around yours reminded me of the child I helped to care for all that time ago. Please forgive me. I must go now. I've disrupted your morning too much already."

She sat looking at me, but her gaze reached far into the distance. Then she spoke.

"Come with me to the cathedral now."

"But madame, there are others who are far better suited to accompanying you than I am."

"No. I wish you to come. Let us go without further delay."

"Yes madame, of course, if that is your wish."

"It is."

She put on a cloak, pulling up the hood to hide her face. She passed another to me.

"Take this and put it on. That way we can both go unnoticed."

As we left the room, I noticed a battered lute case on the chair.

We walked quickly, completing the short distance to the cathedral without attracting unwanted attention and without speaking. After briefly passing the time of day with the verger,

Madame Cecilia graciously hiding her impatience to enter, we hurried up the nave, under the rood screen, to the high altar. She gazed up at the painting and sank to her knees, the hood of her cloak slipping from her head, her long, unpinned hair falling loose just as in the altarpiece. I looked at her. Though she was older and her hair streaked with grey, I knew beyond any doubt that it was she who was depicted as the Virgin. She wept quietly. I knelt beside her and put my arm around her shoulders to comfort her, my own eyes also full of tears. We remained there in silence for some time.

"What is the name of the artist?" she whispered eventually.

"Johannes Peeters," I answered.

"Is he still alive?"

"Yes, madame. He is my master. He lives in Herengracht, near where you are staying."

She began to cry again, burying her face in my shoulder. Then she uttered words that I will never forget.

"He honoured his promise to bring me home. Along the way I abandoned him for the sake of music, but he did what he said he would do – lead us both back to the north where we belonged. Take me to him – now. I must see him. I must thank him."

She paused for a few moments in prayer before the altar, then once more pulled up the hood of her cloak to conceal her tear-stained face. We left the cathedral and came to this house. I took her up to the master's room. She tapped on the door.

"Come in," said the frail voice from within.

She stepped inside.

"It's me, Khadra, your companion, your daughter, Marie Angélique."

I closed the door, tempted to remain outside and eavesdrop, but I knew that would be neither right nor proper, so I left them alone. They were together all day. That evening she performed in the cathedral, where many members of the audience were struck by the uncanny likeness of the composer to the young Virgin in the altarpiece. Afterwards, she returned and I heard her playing the lute to the master and singing. I recognised the song, its bitter-sweet words: "To see, to hear, to touch, to kiss, to die, With thee again in sweetest sympathy." Since then, they have been inseparable. The curtains of this house are now drawn back daily, its silent rooms filled with the sound of joy.

There, my friend. I have brought you up to date. It is said that a woman's heart contains within its small bounds an ocean of secrets. I have shared many of them with you, and it is almost time for you to leave. But before you rise from your chair, there is one more secret I wish to reveal, if you promise not to disclose it to anyone. You do? Well, then.

He is not her father. He believes he is and she believes that too. That is how it must stay. For them to know otherwise would break their hearts. But I can disclose to you that in the early hours of that morning long ago – after the child was born and the master was informed he had a daughter – the midwife confided to Wilhelmina that, in the excruciating pain of her labour, the mistress had cursed the man who had made her conceive. The name she uttered was not the master's.

After the birth, the mistress asked the midwife what she might have said in her distress. The midwife disclosed the name she had condemned to eternal damnation. The mistress forbade her ever to reveal it and later the midwife received a substantial sum of the master's money to ensure her silence. I believe that the child, so long as she was at Herengracht, was a reminder of the secret that haunted the mistress and that this painful fact might possibly have led her to give the child away. I think guilt for what she did tormented her during the remaining years of her life, however hard she tried to forget her actions – bearing a child that was not her husband's and then giving it away to avoid the daily living reminder of her transgression.

There, I have told you all. Now, passer-by, you must go. And it is time for me, too, to leave.

CHAPTER SEVENTEEN

Epilogue

To this day the imposing altarpiece of the Virgin with the Christ Child hangs above the cathedral's high altar, a position it has occupied, with two exceptions, since the removal of the shroud. The work of art was seized by German occupying forces in the early years of World War II and incarcerated in a Bohemian salt mine. Some years after its retrieval at the end of the conflict, it was removed for extensive restoration. Since then, it has dominated the chancel and the apse above it.

Though much admired, it remains controversial as it is so startlingly different in style from the form of religious art prevalent at the beginning of the eighteenth century. The Virgin, as she is portrayed, seems almost three dimensional, as though she is stepping out of the altarpiece's simple gilt frame to greet the viewer. Like some of those at the time of its unveiling, many see the work as a remarkable depiction of reality – not a traditional sacred icon but a vivid representation of the human body, challenging expectations shaped by such stylised, rarefied, idealised religious art. Though little is known about what inspired the artist to paint the image he did, there is still debate as to whether the Virgin is the expression of his paternal love for a long-lost child, visualised here as an adult, or an expression of physical love for a woman who existed only in his imagination, part of a make-believe journey representing his lifelong quest for personal enlightenment. The two side panels have received little comment over the years. Indeed, they were removed for a period in the late-nineteenth century, thus concentrating the altarpiece's visual impact. But after the Great War they were re-joined to the main picture, for the sake of artistic integrity.

As for the artist, he is now forgotten. Occasionally, his portraits, commissioned by clients for display on the walls of family houses, appear on the art market, but rarely raise much interest or value.

And what of the lute player? She inevitably became one of the significant number of female musicians and composers largely overlooked in the robust world of male composers over the past centuries. Like the late-seventeenth-century French composer Élisabeth Jacquet de la Guerre, her musical repertoire is rarely heard these days. Her famous trademark lute disappeared long ago.

The house in Herengracht is still there – much renovated and revelling in the latest design luxury. The *voorhuis* has become a busy IT office. The rooms behind remain *en enfilade* and the windows are now larger, permitting more daylight to penetrate the darker recesses within. Concealed beneath stylish modern wooden flooring are the original tiles of the age. With those exceptions, the house has no evident reminders of the past – other than a small piece of tightly folded yellowed paper, lodged firmly in a crack in the fabric of the house behind some eighteenth-century wood panelling in the dining room, itself hidden behind state-of-the-art sound-proofing, insulating partitioning. If it were ever discovered, the reader would see the following words of Phaedrus:

> *Things are not always what they seem; the first appearance deceives many; the intelligence of few perceives what has been carefully hidden in the recesses of the mind.*

That said, it is indeed often difficult to discern fact from fiction, as in this tale.

AUTHOR'S NOTE

This is my fifth novel in five years and very different from what I have written before.

The first three books, known as the Herzberg trilogy, chronicle the fortunes and vicissitudes of two fictional families – one English, one German, linked by marriage – over a period of 150 years. With an interwoven musical theme, their narrative has as its backdrop the later years of Frederick the Great, the French Revolution, the Napoleonic Wars and Europe's later slide towards the First World War. The third book in the trilogy, *A Motif of Seasons*, describes the painful impact of the rupture in 1914 on both families. What happens to them is emblematic of the irreversible severing of ties that occurred between many families in real life at that time.

Drawing once again on my diplomatic career and knowledge of German history, my fourth book, *The Executioner's House*, leaves the world of the Herzberg trilogy behind to tell of a fictional struggle between British and Soviet intelligence in 1946 war-devastated Berlin and of two people who become unwitting pawns in its conduct.

The Lute Player was inspired by three facts that suddenly came together in my imagination to form a story I wished to write without delay.

The first is that my wife Audrey and I possess a late-sixteenth-century painting of the Adoration of the Magi by an unknown Dutch artist, which depicts in the background a tree-rich landscape, a castle, elephants, camels and horses. We believe from our research that the picture was once part of a larger imposing altarpiece. The second fact is that, whilst visiting an exhibition earlier this year in The Queen's Gallery in London, I unexpectedly saw – and heard – a lute being played; it was a striking instrument with a beguiling sound. The third and decisive fact is the visit Audrey and I made to Jerusalem and Palestine in November 2017 as part of a study group on the occasion of the one hundredth anniversary of the Balfour Declaration.

One afternoon, in Bethlehem, in the shadow of the wall of separation, we met an impressive and charismatic Palestinian woman called Khadra, with whom we spent over two remarkable hours; they included a visit with her to the ancient Church of the Nativity, which is believed to stand on the site of Christ's birthplace. The encounter with Khadra, present-day Bethlehem's resonance with the city depicted in the painting we possess and the sound of the lute – similar to that of the Arab oud – together created for me the irresistible basis for a story I had to write.

So, during the bitter Norfolk winter of February and March this year, I wrote the story, in which even the now notorious "Beast from the East" storm gets a walk-on part.

Edward Glover
North Norfolk
16 July 2018

ACKNOWLEDGEMENTS

I wish to thank several people for their generous assistance, advice and support in writing this book.

First, my warmest thanks go to Jenny Langford, who once again stepped forward to help with my research and to read patiently the raw text of each chapter, spotting errors and inconsistencies. Second, my gratitude goes to my daughter Caroline and her husband Hugo. Both art-restoration experts, they gave me invaluable advice about the early-eighteenth-century process of preparing a canvas for a major art work such as an altarpiece and the long and arduous task of painting the images on it. Their combined input helped me to describe with greater conviction how my fictional artist went about the monumental task he set himself.

Third, this book greatly benefited from the expertise of my copy-editor, Sue Tyley, who, as she did with my previous novels, gave it her highly professional and forensically detailed attention. She has my profound gratitude for another significant contribution. Similar appreciation and thanks go to Niall Cook, the designer of all my books, for creating, as always, so distinctive a cover and preparing the layout and presentation of the contents. He is a much-valued stalwart in my work as an author.

Last but certainly not least, I wish to thank my wife Audrey, my sons Rupert and Crispin, and my other daughter, Charlie, for encouraging me to keep going and ensuring I met the challenge of yet another self-imposed tight deadline despite a backdrop of other, competing preoccupations at the Foreign and Commonwealth Office and elsewhere.

ABOUT THE AUTHOR

Edward Glover was born in London. After gaining a history degree followed by an MPhil at Birkbeck College, London University, he embarked on a career in the British diplomatic service, during which his overseas postings included Washington DC, Berlin, Brussels and the Caribbean. He subsequently advised on foreign ministry reform in post-invasion Iraq, Kosovo and Sierra Leone. For seven years he headed a one-million-acre rainforest-conservation project in South America, on behalf of the Commonwealth Secretariat and the Government of Guyana.

With an interest in 16th- and 18th-century history, baroque music and 18th-century art, in 2012 Edward was encouraged by the purchase of two paintings and a passport to try his hand at writing historical fiction.

Edward and his wife, former Foreign & Commonwealth Office lawyer and leading international human rights adviser Dame Audrey Glover, now live in Norfolk, a place that gives him further inspiration for his writing. He is vice-chairman and director (communication) of the Foreign & Commonwealth Office Association, a trustee of the Welsh environmental charity Size of Wales and of the King's Lynn Preservation Trust, and an associate fellow of the University of Warwick's Yesu Persaud Centre for Caribbean Studies.

When he isn't writing, Edward is an avid tennis player and – at the age of 71 – completed the 2014 London Marathon, raising £7,000 for Ambitious about Autism.